In
Her Father's
Footsteps

Also by
BIANCA BRADBURY

Andy's Mountain
Dogs and More Dogs
Jim and His Monkey
The Loner
Mutt
A New Penny
One Kitten Too Many
The Three Keys
Those Traver Kids
Two on an Island
My Pretty Girl

In Her Father's Footsteps

BIANCA
BRADBURY

Illustrated by Richard Cuffari

Houghton Mifflin Company Boston 1976

Library of Congress Cataloging in Publication Data

Bradbury, Bianca.
  In her father's footsteps.

  SUMMARY: Jenny thought her future as a
veterinarian in partnership with her father was
assured until, beginning with the fire in the
animal hospital, everything went wrong.
  [1. Veterinarians—Fiction] I. Cuffari,
Richard, 1925–   II. Title.
PZ7.B716In   [Fic]   75-43891
ISBN 0-395-24381-5

1

Afterward, Jenny knew that the second week in March was one she would remember forever. It was a real dilly, and it cut her life in two.

Up until Tuesday night it was a perfectly nice, ordinary week. She and her father sat down to dinner at six that night. Mrs. Randall, who came to cook and clean, had left the meal on the stove for Jenny to heat up. Dr. Wren served Jenny's plate, and she was about to ask, "What kind of a day did you have?" when the phone rang.

She was nearest, and got up to answer. Some animal was sick or hurt, and she could take the information for the doctor. A high, excited voice cried, "Jenny? My Muffin won't eat!"

This could only be Mrs. Alice Ferris, who had a bad habit of calling the doctor if her Yorkshire terrier looked at her cross-eyed. Jenny longed to say "So what?" but she didn't. "That doesn't sound too awfully serious," she said. "Maybe he just isn't hungry."

The lady went on to describe the meal her dog had refused, roast beef and fresh peas. Jenny was thinking, Hey, I wish we ate as well! Her father's raised eyebrows were asking what was up, and she mouthed, "Muffin won't eat his roast beef."

1

He frowned with annoyance, then chuckled, got up, and took the receiver. "Mrs. Ferris, give Muffin a message for me," he ordered. "If Muffin doesn't scoff up that roast beef right now, I'll come and give him a dose of castor oil that'll keep him busy for a month. Tell him he's not a sick dog, he's just spoiled rotten. Yes, you can call me tomorrow if he doesn't eat his breakfast."

Dr. Wren hung up. He and Jenny were starting on their meatloaf and scalloped potatoes when the phone rang again. This man didn't fool around; he barked, "Put your father on!" Jenny handed her father the receiver.

Dr. Wren didn't fool around either. "Bring the dog in right away," he ordered, and hung up.

He glanced at the clock. "It'll take them fifteen minutes to get here," he said, and began shoveling in his dinner.

"Who is it?" Jenny asked.

"Ben Briscoe. He brought in one of his hunting dogs this afternoon with what looks like fox mange. This countryside is almost rid of that. The mangy foxes died and those that survived are healthy. But there must be some left in the woods, and Ben's bird dog went for a run and picked it up. I gave Ben the stuff for a dip. It's pretty potent. Ordinarily I'd treat the dog myself, but Ben's knowledgeable, and I figured he'd do the job right. I told him to wait for a sunny, warm day and bathe the dog outside. He didn't; he bathed it when he got home and kept it in the house, and it breathed in the concentrated fumes.

2

Now it's back legs are dragging and it sounds like paralysis."

Dr. Wren pushed back his plate, got up, and grabbed his mackinaw. "Do you need me?" Jenny asked.

"No. I'll have my pie and coffee when I get through."

The car arrived and Jenny watched from the window. To her, the veterinarian business was endlessly fascinating, and she planned to be a vet herself. In fact, all her hopes and dreams were aimed in that direction. The floodlight lit the scene, and she saw the two men struggling to lift the heavy dog. They carried it into the small, white hospital.

Jenny finished her own dinner, did the dishes, and set the coffee pot on a plate turned low. She looked at her chemistry assignment and decided she could master it during her study period the next day. She started reading her English assignment, but she was listening for sounds from the yard.

The hospital door banged, and she went to look. The dog was walking. It staggered along between its master and the doctor, but it was moving under its own power.

Dr. Wren came in, and Jenny served the coffee and cherry pie. "The dog's okay," she commented.

"Yes, it's all right, and I've learned my lesson," he said. "I won't trust anybody with such a powerful dip; I'll treat the dog myself. Hey, this is good," he added.

"Mrs. Randall really makes a neat pie."

"Not as good as your mother did," Dr. Wren said,

then scowled, because it still cost him pain to mention Martha Wren. Jenny's mother had died of cancer two years ago, and her death had left a terrible gap in their lives, which nothing could fill.

Jenny had found some bills in the mail when she came home from school, and had propped them against the bowl of plastic fruit in the middle of the table. The doctor reached for them now. She hated bugging him about bills, but some of these were two months old. Her mother's long illness had left a heavy burden of debt. His scowl deepened. "I paid these," he said.

"I don't believe you did, Daddy," she said gently. "How about the money we borrowed from the bank? Isn't it almost paid off?"

"Almost. We owe under a thousand."

"Dad, I've asked you before to let Mrs. Randall go, and now I'm asking again. We could save quite a wad, and I think she'd welcome the idea. She's dropped hints that she's getting too old to work out."

"You couldn't run the house and keep up your school work."

"Yes, I could. Mrs. Randall only does a little cleaning every day, and cooks our dinner. We could manage. We'd eat TV dinners, and you know you like TV dinners."

"No, we won't talk about it," he said. "You've got to do well in school if you hope to be a vet. You've already got a big load, keeping this house going, and I ought to help you more."

Suiting the action to the word, he gathered up plates

4

and coffee cups and started for the kitchen. Worthless, the black Labrador, must have been lying in the doorway. Worthless yelped and Dr. Wren yelled and the crash shook the house. Jenny rushed out and found her father sprawled on the kitchen floor, with Worthless standing over him, licking his face.

She located his glasses, which had skidded under the sink. "I'm going to be a real help," he said mildly. "I've started off by breaking one of your mother's Haviland cups."

They did the washing-up together. Jenny still had some homework to reckon with, and went to her room. The house was so old it creaked in every joint, and she heard her father come upstairs about ten.

She finished her studying, put on her pajamas, and brushed her long, dark hair. She wore it in two braids, Indian-fashion, because hair was something Jenny refused to fuss with.

Sometimes, like tonight, when her hair was framing her face, it occurred to her that she wasn't too awful looking. Her nose was a nice, slim nose and her dark eyes were okay. Most of the time, though, she thought of herself as an ugly duckling. Anybody as flat-chested as she was didn't have much chance of turning into a raving beauty. If she was ever going to grow any bosom she would have to start soon.

This problem didn't really get her down, but it was all she had on her mind. The night was fairly warm, for March, and she had a struggle opening her window. The old latches put up a real battle. Her room was at the front of the house, and she watched the cars tearing along the state road. She thought, April's coming, and Oh, neat! It'll be spring — .

"Jenny!" her father shouted.

She leaped for the hall and he was there, struggling into his pants. "The hospital's afire!" he yelled.

Through the window of his room she saw the red glow. She started down the stairs. "Jenny, get dressed!" he ordered.

"The animals!"

"There aren't any."

"Daddy, the animals!" she screamed, beside herself with fear.

He seized her and shook her. "Jenny, I tell you, the place is empty! Call the Fire Department, and then get dressed and come!"

She dialed the number. Her father and the Volunteer Fire Department had the same answering service. "It's my dad's hospital!" she yelled. She pulled on pants and a coat and rushed outside.

The doctor was in the office and the spotlight in the yard showed what he was doing. He had shut the door on the back room, where the fire was, but the smoke was awful. He was struggling with the file cabinet, trying to drag it across the floor. She joined him. "Dad, just take the drawers," she suggested.

"Good idea," he said quite calmly. He carried out the first drawer, calling back to her, "Get the instruments."

She grabbed the black record book and the bag on his desk, the one he took on house calls. The instrument cabinet in the surgery was too heavy to be moved, so she piled the surgical instruments into a box. They worked frantically, filling boxes and baskets with books and jars and bottles of medicine. Together they carried out the sterilizer. Choking and coughing they wrestled with the treatment table, trying to get it through the door. Then the fire truck swooped into the yard, siren shrieking. Suddenly the place was swarming with men, and there was nothing more they could do.

They stood on the frozen grass, watching. The fire burst out of the back room, the ward, where the animal cages were. It engulfed the surgery, and soon the office and the waiting room filled with flame. The men played water on the roof and into the fiery interior, but it was clear the little hospital was doomed. One fireman asked, "How about the animals?"

"There weren't any here, thank God," Dr. Wren told him.

"Dad, are you absolutely sure?" Jenny asked.

"I'm sure," he said. "Hokie Jones was here this afternoon when Mrs. Parsons came for her dog, and Miss Horowitz collected her cat. Another cat was hit in the road this morning, but it wasn't badly hurt, and the owner showed up to claim it."

How could he be so calm? Tears were running down Jenny's face because it seemed to her she was watching her father's whole life go down the drain. He had built the place with his own hands twenty years ago, when he first set up private practice.

The neighbors had gathered. Bundled up in coats over their night clothes they silently watched, like

7

mourners. The fire was eating through the roof, and everyone moved back as the roof collapsed and the walls caved in with a dreadful, dull roar. "She's a total loss, Doc," the fire chief said. "Have you any idea what set it off?"

"None at all," Dr. Wren told him.

"Probably wiring. I sure hope you had enough insurance."

Jenny stood beside the pathetic pile of things they had rescued. The fire was still hot on her face but she was shaking with chills, and her father put his arms around her. The firemen continued to pour water into the glowing pile until the chief called, "Never mind, boys. The Doc's better off with a heap of ashes instead of a lot of burned timbers. Where do you want your stuff, Doc? My boys will move it."

Neighbors helped too, carrying what the Wrens had rescued into the woodshed. Then the doctor suggested, "Jen, suppose you go in the house and make coffee."

"Don't bother, Jen," said Mr. Osborne, who lived next door. "Coffee's ready at our house."

Mrs. Osborne clucked over Jenny like a mother hen, then served coffee and doughnuts to the firemen who crowded into her kitchen. They were joking and laughing, but watching the Wrens sympathetically.

Dr. Wren was very popular in Harley. He wasn't the most successful vet, money-wise, but he was probably the most popular. One way or another, Jenny realized, he had done favors for most of the men who had turned out to fight his fire. Before they left they all managed to shake his hand and say, "Too bad, Doc. I'm sorry, Doc."

She was surprised to see that the clock said one. Had only two hours elapsed? "You'd better take this girl home," Mr. Osborne suggested to the doctor. "She looks like she's about done in."

Jenny meekly followed her father across the yard. The firemen and the neighbors were all gone. What had been the hospital was a pile of ash and a few timbers, fitfully glowing. Jenny paused, and her father said, "Honey, let's not look at it any more tonight."

They wearily climbed the stairs. "Dad," Jenny began.

"Not now," he said. "There's a lot to talk about, but it can wait until morning."

She felt grimy and smoky, and stumbled into the bathroom. She gave the mirror only a quick glance while she scrubbed with a soapy cloth, but it seemed to her she looked a lot older now than the last time she had looked, earlier in the evening.

2

She awoke in the gray dawn wondering what the odd smell was. Then she realized that the smell of smoke was in her hair, and remembered that the pretty, white hospital was gone. She couldn't get up the gumption to face this new day. Tears slipped down her face, tears for her father, and she thought about his life.

He had made himself a good life. He had put himself through college and vet school. He had married Jenny's mother, and that was just about the best thing that could happen to any man. He had come to Harley in answer to an ad in a professional journal. Dr. James Everts had needed an assistant. Darling old Dr. Everts, he was still alive and still practicing.

After a while Dr. Tom had figured he ought to strike out on his own. Dr. Everts had loaned him the money to put down a payment on the Spicer place, this lovely old house on the state road, and to build his modest hospital.

Jenny lay with her arms under her head, staring at the cracked ceiling. Poor Dad, she thought. I hate to think how he'll feel when he looks out and sees that pile of ashes.

She was still reviewing the family history. Her father sincerely believed that practicing veterinary medicine was the finest profession in the world. He did well and built up a practice and paid off his debts.

So, she thought, I came along. We had a great life, we really did. How many kids can honestly say they had a happy childhood? Until Mom died.

Whenever she recalled that nightmarish time, Jenny's mind closed down as though a heavy curtain were drawn. The sickroom at home, the trips to the hospital, the pain and ugliness, her mother's unbelievable courage, the awful, awful loss at the end.

Time healed, yes, it did. The trite saying was true.

She heard the click of Worthless's claws on the stairs, and he pushed open the door and stuck his nose in Jenny's face. He was telling her that she had jolly well better let him out if she didn't want to clean up a large, dog-made lake. "I get the message," she told him.

The house was damp, chilly. The ancient furnace was inadequate and the Wrens couldn't afford a new one. Jenny pulled on wool pants and a heavy sweater and followed Worthless downstairs, yawning.

The three house cats were anxiously milling around the kitchen. She opened the door and they streaked past her. Light snow had fallen, and that was good. It hid the ugly pile. Worthless set out on his morning run through the neighbor's yards, but he paused to sniff around the disaster area. A thin plume of smoke still rose from one corner.

The first order of business was to start the coffee, then make breakfast for the cats. In a few minutes the three regulars plus five or six freeloaders would be shrieking for food. There were too many but what could the Wrens do? These waifs and strays didn't march up and knock on the door, they were dropped along the state road by cruel slobs in cars.

Jenny mixed dry food with water and added cat tuna. The coffee pot perked out a perfume that would wake up the doctor. Jenny wanted the cats out of the way before he came down; it discouraged him when he realized how many he was supporting. She filled plates, set them on newspapers, and opened the door. The mob rushed in as though this was going to be their last meal on earth. They were a good-natured bunch, and took time from their greedy eating to give Jenny appreciative glances. They considered her a really great cook.

She heard her father on the stairs. "Your coffee wakes a man out of a sound sleep," he complained.

She opened the back door and the cats, replete and satisfied, marched out to start their day of exploring and adventure. "Sit down, Pa," Jenny ordered, and gave him his coffee.

He blinked at her. "You're not dressed for school."

"No," she said. "Remember? We had a bit of excitement last night. We have to begin to think how we're going to cope."

They heard a honking in the road. Jenny stepped outside and waved to the bus driver to go on. Kids were staring, and Thursa Poniatowski, Jenny's best friend, waved back at her.

14

Jenny shut the door. "Do you want some eggs?" she asked.

"Not now," her father said. "I did some thinking last night. I didn't sleep too well. Now I have no place to practice, so my income stops. There's only one good thing — "

"I know," Jenny broke in. "It was the mercy of God there weren't any animals in those cages."

"Right. What if the Parsonses' dog had burned? That mutt is the light of their lives."

"Did you come to any conclusions, when you were doing all that thinking?" Jenny asked.

"No, but I have a few ideas. For instance, I could take a job, to tide us over."

"What kind of a job?"

"Oh, I don't know. On an assembly line, maybe. They say the pay's good. Or I could work in an office."

"Doing what?"

"Keeping books. I'm pretty fair at figures."

She stared at him, astonished. "Frankly, Daddy, I've always thought you were the world's worst bookkeeper," she said. "If you got that kind of a job you'd be fired the first week."

"You don't respect your father."

"Oh yes, I do. But a businessman you ain't!"

They laughed. All their lives they had quarreled easily and laughed easily together. "Old Doc would take me into his practice, but I owe that man too much already," Dr. Wren went on.

15

"You can't ask Uncle Jim," Jenny agreed. "How about the Golden Boys, though? I've heard they're looking for a third vet to join their wonderful clinic."

She was referring to Dr. Simon Winters and Dr. Walter Ziller, two ambitious, young veterinarians who had set up practice in Harley. It was kind of ominous, the way they were cornering the business. One thing was sure, they didn't include the deadbeats among their clients. The deadbeats were a loyal crowd and stuck with Dr. Everts and Dr. Wren.

"I don't believe I could work with them," Dr. Wren said. "I've been my own man too long. The first time we disagreed about a case I'd either have to knuckle under or I'd have to walk out."

"Right on," Jenny said. "Besides that, you'd have a tough time convincing yourself that making a pile of money is what it's all about." She got up. "Now I'm going to fix you a decent breakfast. We don't know what this day may bring forth, and we've got to be ready for it."

His voice shook. "You sound like your mother," he said. "She always figured that when people were in trouble the first thing they had to do was to eat. All right, we'll have breakfast, and then I'll gird up my loins. That was another expression I got from her, I guess. I'll gird up my loins and go to see the insurance people."

He ate, then went upstairs and changed into a real suit, a white shirt, and a tie. This was a sign of how important he considered the coming interview, be-

16

cause he usually slopped around in flannel shirts, boots, and old jackets.

Jenny had inherited her fondness for sloppy dressing from him. Small, pretty Martha Wren had always looked as though she had stepped out of the proverbial bandbox, but dressing up had never been Jenny's bag.

She held his sheepskin jacket, gave her father a pat, and watched him go. The garage was part of the long ell connected to the rear of the house. He backed carefully, making sure he didn't run over any cats. Worthless planted himself in the car's path, and Dr. Tom stopped and Worthless clambered in.

What to do, what to do? Jenny wondered. She washed the dishes, made the beds, thought about doing some dusting but gave up the idea because Mrs. Randall had cleaned the day before.

She made one resolution: Mrs. Randall would have to go. The way the situation looked to Jenny, money was going to be very, very tight.

The phone rang. Miss Douglas was on duty at the answering service. "Jenny, why aren't you in school?" she demanded. "Oh, I know, you stayed home on account of the fire. Tell your daddy to call Mrs. Sheldon on River Street. Her dog's limping. I'm glad she wants your pa, because lately she's been giving her business to the fancy new doctors."

"Do you take their calls, too?" Jenny asked.

"Sure do; we're the only answering service in town. Also will you remind the doctor he's supposed to go up Ore Mountain way today to finish testing the Polaskis' cows?"

"Thanks, Miss Douglas."

"I'm sorry about your trouble."

"Thanks, Miss Douglas."

Jenny felt warmed by the contact. Harley was growing fast, turning into a bedroom town for Moss City, fifteen miles away, but it still kept many of its small-town ways. The last phrase of Miss Douglas's was familiar; it was what people had said when Martha Wren died. They had taken Dr. Wren's hand or put their arms around Jenny and said, "I'm sorry about your trouble." It was the truth; when Harley people had trouble, other people did feel sorry.

I'm sorry about our trouble too, Jenny thought now, staring out the back door. She wished the thin snow would never melt, because it glossed over the ugly heap of ashes.

The phone rang again. "This is Eve Simmons," a musical voice announced. "Jenny, will you tell your father I've heard the news, and I won't expect him tonight?"

"All right, Mrs. Simmons."

"It's Miss Simmons," the caller said, and thanked Jenny and hung up.

Miss Eve Simmons, who was she? Jenny placed her then. She taught in the middle school. Probably she had an ailing animal and Dr. Wren had offered to make a house call because she couldn't bring it in during office hours. But why hadn't she mentioned her dog or her cat or whatever it was?

18

3

When Dr. Wren came home, the droop of his shoulders showed that the news wasn't good. He stamped the snow off his shoes and hung his coat on a doorknob. Jenny told him about his calls. "The Sheldons' dog is limping," she said. "Miss Douglas says they've been going to Winters and Ziller. You don't have to take their castoffs."

"A nice setter like the Sheldons' isn't anybody's castoff," Dr. Wren said. "What are the other calls?"

"There was a Davis. Here's the number. And Miss Douglas says you're supposed to finish that herd you were testing, up on Ore Mountain."

Dr. Wren grinned. "Anna may not realize it, but her nosiness saves me from having to hire a private secretary."

"A Miss Simmons called," Jenny told him.

He made no comment. He stuck the slip of paper with the numbers in his shirt pocket, then hunched over, brooding. "Well?" Jenny asked.

"I didn't make out too well," he admitted. "Carl Kaplan warned me some time ago I was under-insured. All I had on the hospital was ten thousand dollars. We'll collect the whole amount because that

19

pile of nothing out there is a total loss. But ten thousand won't go far toward replacing it."

"It sounds like a lot," Jenny said.

"It isn't, when you consider the cost of lumber and the wages workmen get nowadays."

They brooded together for awhile. Clearly her father couldn't wrestle with his problems, right now. Jenny played along. "Did anything else interesting happen?" she asked.

"I met your Uncle Jim on the stairs in the bank building. That's an awful set of stairs, and I reminded him he's had one heart attack. He ordered me not to tell you because he didn't need a scolding from you. I think he'd been up to see Carl, to ask how much fire insurance I carried. He wanted to know because he intends to bail us out."

"You think he's going to offer you a loan?"

"I know he is. He asked me to drop in on him this afternoon. The trouble is, he'd call it a loan but he'd mean it as a gift. We can't start building up new indebtedness."

"Okay," Jenny said, "but when he offers, Daddy, refuse it gently. He's sensitive these days. He still feels bad about Mom, and he still misses his own wife, after ten years. Let's have him for supper soon.

"There's somebody else we have to consider, and that's Hokie Jones," she went on. "He's so kind of self-effacing, we forget about him. Maybe you could give him a ring tonight. He's always working around here, and he won't take any money, so we have to let him know that we appreciate."

"Good idea," her father agreed, patting the top of her head as he went to the phone.

Mrs. Davis's cat needed spaying, and he explained that he had lost his business overnight and suggested she call Dr. Everts. Then he departed to make his house calls. Jenny watched him go. There wasn't much bulk to him, but there was a lot of strength in him. He would need it if he faced a morning of wrestling cattle, although the Polaskis would help him.

There was something Jenny wanted to know. How much stuff had she and her father actually rescued last night? She put on a warm coat and went to look.

The firemen had arranged the boxes and stuff in the woodshed beyond the garage. It wasn't a big pile. The roof of the ell was tight, but the woodshed had a dirt floor. These things were the tools of Tom Wren's trade, and it would be a disaster if the books mildewed and the instruments rusted. Jenny found a plastic sheet and tucked it around the sterilizer. She wiped off the books. Everything would have to be cleaned and stored in a clean, dry place.

She screwed up her courage then and went to take a real look at the hospital area. The snow had melted, so the ugliness was laid bare. She took a stick and poked around in the ashes and charred timbers. The waiting-room furniture was destroyed. The refrigerator lay on its side, a complete loss. The treatment table looked hopeless too, bent out of kilter, the legs twisted. Maybe the cages from the ward could be salvaged. She found little else.

She puttered around for the rest of the day. It

seemed important that she fix a good dinner. Mrs. Randall sometimes made red-flannel hash and the doctor loved it. Jenny boiled some potatoes, fried a chopped onion, chopped a can of corned beef and the potatoes together coarsely, and let the whole mess brown slowly.

She was sniffing the elegant smell when somebody called, "Hey, Jenny Wren!" Sam, the Osbornes's nine-year-old, was at the door. "I brought Worthless home," he said, handing her a rope with a black dog at the end of it.

"Why?" she asked. "All he had to do was walk across the yard."

"My mother wants you and your father to come for supper."

"That's awfully nice of her, but I've already fixed supper," Jenny told him.

Sam hung around. He liked the Wren house because this was where the action was; people were always rushing into the yard with interesting emergencies. Only last night the Wrens had provided the neighborhood with a first-class fire. "You can't stay," Jenny told him. "I have to clear the decks before my father comes. Will you go home if I give you two cookies?"

"How about three?"

"All right, three, but that's blackmail." Jenny wrote a note for his mother, and he took his cookies and left.

Dr. Wren looked more cheerful than Jenny expected when he appeared in the early twilight. He sniffed, and Jenny said, "Yes, it's corned beef hash.

Mrs. Osborne invited us, but I asked her for a rain check."

"I was planning to invite you out for dinner," her father said.

"Where to?"

"The Brass Lantern."

"That means dressing up," Jenny said. "Besides, I've fixed this good hash."

"I was also going to take you to Moss City to a movie."

"Dad, you're nuts," Jenny said. "You never go to the movies."

"It's time I started, then."

"Dad, it costs three dollars. Each. And you don't know what movies are like nowadays. If it's sex, you'd die because it's all there in living color, and if it's cops and robbers it's awfully bloody — ."

She stopped because he had an odd look on his face. "Somebody else is going with us," he said. "I sort of invited Eve Simmons."

"You what?" Jenny said, startled.

"I invited Miss Simmons. She'd like you to come with us."

"No, thanks, I guess not," Jenny said.

"Why not?"

"Well, I don't really want to get dressed up."

What did she expect him to say? "All right, if you don't want to go, then we'll call it off." He didn't. He said, "I hope you'll save me some of that hash; it smells great," and then he went upstairs.

She heard him moving around up there. She was

thinking hard. In the two years since Martha had died, not once had he showed any interest in any woman. Oh, it had occurred to Jenny that he might, some day. But now that day had apparently arrived, and this really set her right back on her heels.

She had always thought of her own career as tied up with her father's, that was the fact. That future was assured. On the day she was born her Uncle Jim Everts had opened a savings account for her, entitled, "Jenny's College." A bachelor uncle on her mother's side had left her a small legacy, and that went into the account. Her mother and father had put in bits and pieces of money. During Martha's long illness, the doctor had refused to touch that account and had borrowed money instead.

All Jenny had to do was to get herself into a good vet school, hang in there, and graduate. She would come back to Harley, and she and her father would be partners. She doubted she would ever get married. She only wanted to be Dr. Jenny Wren, Dr. Tom's old-maid partner in the horse, cow, cat, and dog business.

This was the life she had planned since she was a little girl. Was that future going up in smoke?

Jenny got hold of herself then. This was nonsense. Her future wasn't going up in smoke just because her father was taking a woman out to dinner.

She was cheerful when he came down. He had put on a white shirt and a tie for the second time today, which was kind of startling. "I hope you have a nice time," Jenny told him.

"I wish you were coming." He sounded really

troubled. "I won't be late. I'll take your tip about the movie; I wouldn't want to expose Eve to all that sex and blood you were telling about. I'll get home early, and you and I can have a talk then."

Left alone, she ate her supper. She called Thursa, and they had a long chat. Then she took a bath and washed her hair.

She was in the kitchen, heating water for a cup of bouillon, when her father arrived home. It was only nine o'clock. "I'll have a cup too," he said.

She got down another mug and fixed it. "Did you have a nice time?" she asked.

"Fine."

"Good dinner?"

"Fine."

"Good company?"

"Fine," he said with a grin.

"You're a communicative clam," she told him. "All right, now. I guess the time has come for us to have a real talk. I'll give you my ideas, okay? First, though, I'd like to know how much we still owe on Mom's hospital bills."

"It's just under a thousand," Dr. Wren told her. "That's down from the five thousand I borrowed from the bank."

"Great," Jenny said. "Here's how I feel, then. We won't have much money coming in, only dribs and drabs. We'll let Mrs. Randall go. That'll save a hundred and twenty-five a month."

"I just can't see it," Dr. Wren said, sounding stubborn. "It would put too heavy a burden on you. It's terribly important that you do well in school, Jen. You have to keep your grades in the A's, especially in your science courses. You've got to get into a first-rate college if you hope to go into veterinary medicine."

"Right," Jenny agreed.

"Why are you so set on it, Jenny? You've grown up in this house, so you know it's a tough profession. It's a bloody damn business and there are an awful lot of heartaches in it."

"I happen to love animals too."

They stirred their bouillon. Probably both were remembering how often in the last few years Jenny had stood by and assisted, holding an animal lovingly while the doctor gave it the needle that put it mercifully to sleep, helping him when a leg had to be set or a wound stitched, sharing in the bloody clean-up afterward. "All right, daughter," Dr. Wren said finally. "I have to admit you're good. Old Doc agrees that apparently you're born for the work. We won't argue about that. I'll still argue, though, about letting Mrs. Randall go."

"No," Jenny said, "because there's that other angle I mentioned. Her husband's retired now on a good pension, and they don't need the money. I honestly think she wants to quit, but she figures we can't get along without her."

"If that's the case, all right," Dr. Wren said. "We won't let it bug us if the house isn't immaculate. And I'll help with the meals, and the wash-up, and I'll try to be more thoughtful. Will you talk to her? I'm no good at that sort of thing."

4

School day mornings were usually bedlam, and that Thursday was no exception. People knew that Dr. Tom was an early riser, so the telephone began to ring at seven. Jenny let Worthless out, fed the mob of cats and put them out, and all the time she was falling over her father. He couldn't answer the telephone in a dignified manner; he sprawled horizontally, scrawling notes and grunting into the receiver.

Jenny cooked his breakfast. Then she braided her hair and gathered up her books. She was General Wren this morning, and issued her father his marching orders. "First thing, Dad, I want you to bring in all the stuff from the hospital. You can store it in the downstairs bedroom. It can't be left in the woodshed one more day."

He looked at her over his coffee cup. "Your mother led me around by the nose, but she had an iron hand in a velvet glove. You've got the iron hand, all right, Jen."

"In a wool mitten," she said, and flipped it at him and closed the door.

The bus was arriving, yellow lights flashing, as Jenny raced down the driveway. She flung herself aboard. The passengers always watched this event with interest, and a senior boy said, "Well done, Jenny Wren."

Thursa Poniatowski had saved a seat for her. Thursa was short, blond, chubby, wide-faced. She patted Jenny's knee happily, all set for a good gossip. They didn't get much of a chance to talk, though, because the other kids crowded around to hear about the Wrens' disaster. Jenny and Thursa parted company when they reached school because Thursa was taking a general course while Jenny was on a college track.

Jenny was a bright girl and knew it; she wasn't exactly a shrinking violet. The mysteries of trig and physics and Chemistry II unfolded easily for her, and things like languages and English were duck soup. She breezed through the day and took a written test in physics, faking what she wasn't sure of.

A dozen times she had to recount the story of the fire. Mr. Aiken, her counselor, stopped her after her last class to express his sympathy. Thursa was down the hall bawling, "Hurry up!"

"I have to run, Mr. Aiken," Jenny said.

"You'll live longer if you stop running, Jenny," he warned, and let her go.

The tide of yellow buses was flowing out of the parking lot. Thursa spotted good old #141 and pulled Jenny into line. Somebody else took her other arm.

Hokie was weird looking, skinny as a willow wand, and so shy the kids figured he spent his private life under a rock. Some even claimed he was retarded, but that was ridiculous because a person couldn't be retarded when his IQ was up near the genius level.

He peered at Jenny through his thick glasses and shook her elbow. "Hokie, I can't miss my bus," she protested.

"I'm riding with you. I want to see your father."

Jenny was the only person at Harley High who really knew Hokie, and that was because he had attached himself to Dr. Wren. He came after school and on weekends and cleaned cages, washed floors, and held animals while they were being treated. He clucked at cats and dogs in a friendly way through the wire cages. He cheerfully did the most menial jobs. As a matter of fact he was making himself indispensable, and this worried the Wrens because he wouldn't even discuss taking money. The Joneses were loaded. Homer Simms Jones, Senior, was chief stockholder in the town's only industry, a steel-rolling mill.

Hokie stood in the aisle, towering over the girls. Jenny was feeling guilty because she should have called him yesterday. A white lie might make him happy, so she said, "Hoke, I'm sorry I couldn't reach you. I called last night but your line was busy."

He probably saw through that; he was smarter than Jenny, a straight A student while Jenny struggled along on A minuses. He seemed pleased, though, that she cared enough to make up a lie. "That's okay," he said. "I've been wondering what your father plans to do."

"We're not sure," she told him. "If you've got any bright ideas we'll be glad to hear them."

He turned away so he wouldn't overhear the girls'

conversation, and they put their heads together for the rest of the trip. Jenny mentioned that the Wrens were letting their part-time housekeeper go. "Good!" Thursa exclaimed. "I can help you. I'll get off at your house."

"Not today," Jenny contradicted. "Everything's in a real hassle."

"Whenever you want me, then," Thursa said, her feelings not hurt by the rebuff.

Pale afternoon sun was slanting across the yard when Jenny and Hokie stood beside the ugly mound, all that was left of the hospital. She was horrified to see tears slipping out from under his glasses. He mopped them away. "I feel terrible," he muttered.

"We saved some stuff," she told him. "I asked Pa to move it but I wouldn't gamble on his remembering."

She was wrong, though. They found the woodshed empty. The doctor had piled the sterilizer and the boxes in the downstairs bedroom, so the smoky smell was in the house now. Jenny flipped open the top of one box. Dr. Tom had carefully wiped the instruments and stored them in plastic bags.

She and Hokie perched on the edge of the bed, brooding on all that was left of a thriving practice. It occurred to Jenny that Hokie might know a lot about that practice. "Hoke, do you know how Dad keeps his books and records?" she asked.

"No, not really. Once in a while he asks me to find a card on a particular case and make a note."

"He doesn't like having anybody poking into his

31

books. Maybe he isn't a very good accountant," Jenny said carefully.

"Maybe not, but the files he keeps on the animals are meticulous."

Jenny rolled that neat word around in her mind. She would have to try using it.

"I would never look into his account books, but I imagine they would show what the whole town knows," Hokie went on. "A lot of people owe him money, and he doesn't make any real attempt to collect it. Was that what you had in mind?"

She nodded.

"What is he doing about his calls?"

"He's handling them as best as he can, making house calls, sending Old Doc the cases that need surgery."

"Dr. Everts's eyes aren't as good as they might be."

"Probably Dad will give him a hand, if it's a tricky case."

"How is your father taking this?"

"He's putting up a good front," Jenny said. "Actually I think he's real beat down."

The kitchen door suddenly opened, and the doctor switched on the lights because early March dusk was falling. He didn't look startled when the two emerged from the bedroom, and the thought crossed Jenny's mind that this wasn't very complimentary. A normal parent would leap to conclusions!

Hokie was so afraid of intruding on people, he usually didn't linger. This time he made no move to leave, and Jenny said, "I'll make coffee."

"Hokie, I was hoping you'd show up," the doctor said. "Wasn't it lucky we got rid of those two animals that afternoon?"

"Yes, sir." Hokie figured his elders were entitled to "sir." "How about the Fowlers' German shepherd?" he asked. "That was a real sick dog."

"It's coming along. You remember, we treated it for poisoning because the symptoms fitted. I still think that was it, although the Fowlers have no reason to suspect any of their neighbors."

"How about that Siamese cat with the low blood count, sir?"

"It's hanging in there. I wish I could transfuse it, but unfortunately there isn't any blood bank for cats."

Hokie's next question was right to the point. "When are you planning to start rebuilding, sir?"

"I don't know."

"Did you get any estimates today?" Jenny asked.

"Yes, I did, Jen, and I wish you'd hurry up with that coffee."

Jenny poured it and stood at the sink with her cup. "Sit down, take a load off your feet!" the doctor barked. She hastened to obey. "I sure enough got the estimates," he said. "I talked to four builders and told them roughly what we need: three fair-sized rooms plus a small office, plus a lavatory, and a storage closet. The lowest estimate was thirty thousand, six hundred."

"Thirty thousand dollars?" Jenny cried.

"Thirty thousand dollars."

The doctor turned to Hokie. "I was badly under-

33

insured. I may be the greatest vet that ever came down the pike, but I'm also the worst businessman. Which is a fact my daughter doesn't hesitate to point out."

"Oh, come off it!" Jenny exclaimed. "I never said that."

"The suggestion was there."

"I'm sure any bank would jump at the chance to loan you the money," Hokie put in.

"Maybe. But have you inquired about interest rates lately, Hokie? I was so shocked my eyeteeth were jarred loose."

There was a pause. Probably both Wrens reached the same conclusion — that their money trouble was a family problem; it wasn't Hokie's. He was so sensitive he got this message and stood up. He was even skinnier than the doctor; an ounce of fat on his bean-pole frame would have been an improvement. The eyes magnified by his thick glasses beamed affectionate good will, and the Wrens smiled up at him. "I'd better go along," he said. "I just want to say, though, that my father asked me to find out if he can help. I think he meant that he'll be happy to make you a loan." Hokie flipped his long muffler around his neck a couple of times and headed for the door.

"Wait!" Dr. Wren ordered. "I'll take you home."

A blast of cold air rushed in. "No need, sir; I'll do my jogging," Hokie said. They heard his big feet pounding down the driveway.

5

The idea came to Jenny in the night when Worthless burrowed under the covers and woke her. She thought, Maybe we don't need a new hospital. Maybe we can use the ell.

It seemed like the middle of the night, but while she was hugging the dog for mutual warmth she heard the clock bong five times. She might as well start the day, get the show on the road. She pushed off the protesting dog, got up, and dressed. Hannibal followed her downstairs, meowing for breakfast.

She let Worthless out and then an impulse seized her; she grabbed her coat and ran after him. Worthless knew this game and took off toward the fields beyond the back yards. She couldn't catch him because nobody could out-run a Labrador retriever, and besides she had to wait for the cats, who were pursuing her in full cry. She slowed down to let them catch up.

This big field, dotted with cedars, sloped to a depression in the center. So far it had survived the invasion of the housing development that edged it all around. Jenny had named the depression after herself, Jenny's Hollow. Worthless was there waiting when she came up. Here she withdrew from the world to do her thinking. Here she also played that she was an Indian in a land not yet invaded by white men. When she lay on the ground, civilization dropped away and the view was empty.

She didn't usually play games at five-thirty of a cold March morning. Harley folk would take a dim view of a girl who sought solitude at such a place at such an hour. She laid down on the wet ground in her heavy coat, and Worthless thumped his tail and planted himself in the crook of her arm. The cats sniffed her delicately and snuggled too. She stared up at the star-filled sky, turning gray now in the east.

Maybe she was a changeling, she thought. Surely she had some Indian blood, she looked so different from her parents. She was dark and heavy-boned; they were fair and lightly built. Also, there was something queer in her that made her want to bolt sometimes, and run and run.

She got up, dusted off her coat, and walked soberly home accompanied by her menagerie. The kitchen felt like the inside of a damp icebox. Wasn't spring ever going to arrive? She lit the oven to take off the chill, then fed the animals and took a peek at her chemistry assignment to make sure she wouldn't get a nasty surprise if the teacher sprang a fast quiz. It was still only six o'clock. She spent a pleasant hour tidying the tool drawer, sorting tools and screws and nails.

Her father hit the deck at seven. He acted uncertain, as though he didn't know what to do with himself, now that his job had been pulled out from under him. Soon they would begin collecting a new set of worries, as the bills piled up — . "Dad, I believe I've got an answer," Jenny began.

"Oh?" He leaned back. Her mother had warned him a thousand times about teetering in the Hitchcock chairs and Jenny longed to do so now, but resisted. "Dad, maybe we don't have to put up a new hospital," she said. "How about this? Let's try this on for size. Rebuilding the ell. It's good, tight construction. Well, we know how they built in those days; they didn't fool around. They used big timbers and pegged them together. We could divide the garage and get our waiting room and surgery out of it. We could use the rest of the ell for the ward and maybe split that too. We never liked having the cages for the cats and dogs in the same room because the dogs scare the cats. We might also put a couple of runs off the end."

"Hmmm," the doctor said.

"Is that all you've got to say?"

"I don't think it would work."

"Why wouldn't it work?" He didn't answer, and she got mad. "It wouldn't work because I thought of it, and I'm a woman, so automatically it's a dumb idea!" she shouted.

"You're not a woman, you're just a kid!" he shouted back.

She wished she had a fast come-back but couldn't think of one. While she fed him and tidied the kitchen, she waited for his comment on her idea. But she had to go off to school finally without his having made one.

The day passed uneventfully, leaving her plenty of

37

time for thinking. Her father had blandly ignored her suggestion. Was that the way it would be when they set up practice together? Would she spend her life agreeing, "Yes, Papa; you're right, Papa?"

Nothing was said at dinner that night. He told about joining his cronies for lunch at a restaurant in town. He stuck around and wiped the dishes.

Jenny was mixed up in her own mind about what women's liberation was, exactly. An equal shake, right? Well, to Jenny this meant that her ideas should be respected. She had laid out what seemed to her a logical answer to their problem. As the evening wore on and her father failed to mention it, she got madder. She watched part of a hockey game, then left abruptly and went to her room.

Saturday dawned warm. Sleeping late was a luxury Jenny couldn't afford because if the kitchen light didn't go on at six the outside cats would start to fight under Dr. Wren's window. Jenny straggled down, fixed the food, and invited the mob in.

They flowed by like a river of multi-colored fur. She stood sniffing. Rose lit the east. She caught a new odor, not just the smell of charred timber. It was the earthy scent of spring, that was what it was, a promise of better times a-coming.

She watched her cats contentedly filling their bellies and thought deeply. She decided one thing. It didn't matter if her father thought she was a belligerent female. She was going to start making order out of this chaos.

He took the wind out of her sails, however, when he

appeared. He accepted his coffee, then said, "By the way, daughter, I called Mark Steen and Eben Caulfield last night after you went upstairs. Eben's an independent contractor, and Steen works for Howard Lumber. They gave the lowest estimates when I asked about putting up a new building. They're coming this morning. I told them we had a new idea, to use the ell. I hope it doesn't hurt your militant soul because I said 'we.' I have to hang onto some tattered shreds of my male chauvinism!"

She grinned and let that crack pass. Breakfast was a cheerful affair.

Thursa came. They wasted only five minutes sitting and gossiping, that was all Thursa would spare for such idle pastimes. She had a nugget to offer; her older sister worked as a waitress at the Brass Lantern. "She was surprised when your dad walked in with Miss Simmons," Thursa mentioned. "She's nice. I had her for English, in middle school." Jenny didn't rise to the bait and made no answer.

Thursa hauled out the vacuum cleaner and went to work. In the Poniatowski home, dirt was a mortal enemy. Jenny didn't mind dirt that much, she could take it or leave it. Just the same it was pleasant to hear the vacuum cleaner shrieking and know that her work was getting done for her.

Mr. Steen came. Dr. Wren went out, but Jenny didn't join them. Her father would begin to think, "Pushy, pushy."

A pickup truck drove in, the back of it full of wailing kids, and a harassed-looking man jumped out. The kids were bending over something, and a hair-raising howl told Jenny it was a dog far gone in pain. Dr. Wren came in, grabbed his old black bag, and told Jenny, "Get the children into the house."

She had a way with small children, and these came at her call. She sat them down at the kitchen table and brought out the cookie jar. The oldest girl joined Jenny at the window. "Our father didn't mean to but he ran over it," she said dully. "It's our collie dog. We've had her for ten years, and her insides are all crushed."

The howl stopped abruptly; the collie's agony was over. The doctor came to the door asking for a blanket to cover the body. Too many similar emergencies in the past had used up Jenny's supply of old blankets and sheets. She handed him some feed bags. The father wrung Dr. Wren's hand and piled his family into the cab of the truck and went home to bury his dog.

Apparently Thursa had been watching from the living room window, and she too was crying. She didn't understand that things like this went on all the time. "Don't let Dad see you crying," Jenny warned. "He hates it when he has to put an animal down. If he was a vet for a thousand years he would never get used to it."

The day went back to normal. There wasn't even any blood to be cleaned up in the driveway as there often was after one of these emergencies. Dr. Wren finished his talk with Mr. Steen, and just as Steen was departing the other contractor appeared.

Jenny watched the men talking, feeling soft as butter toward her father. How many girls had a dad who could help bring live animals into the world, a litter of pups, a calf, a foal? Who could cure sickness and set broken bones and dig out bullets? Who could perform truly delicate surgery on tangled-up insides? Who could give an animal suffering intolerable pain the wonderful gift of an easy death?

This was one of those moments of revelation when Dr. Wren looked to his daughter like a man fifteen feet tall. Was there any better calling? Ministering to humans? Yes, maybe, although Jenny wasn't absolutely sure that this was so. I'll settle for being a vet, she promised herself. Someday she too would have a sign swinging on the wrought-iron post in the front yard. "Jenny Wren, D.V.M."

"Hey, Jen, come on out!" Dr. Wren broke in on her musing.

The men were in the catch-all beyond the woodshed. Eben Caulfield, a wiry grasshopper of a man, was hopping up and down to keep warm. "Eben thinks it can be done," the doctor told Jenny.

"How about the cost?" she asked. "That other figure — thirty thousand, six hundred — that's just too rich for our blood."

Mr. Caulfield chuckled. "That wasn't my figure, Jenny, that was Mark Steen's. I told your dad thirty thousand even."

"Six hundred less, that's not much," she pointed out. "What will we save if we re-build the ell?"

"I can't give you an answer straight out," he said.

"The other was easy, we just figure so much per square foot of space. Now this ell — the roof's good, the frame's sound. Those boys who built it two hundred years ago did a beautiful job. The wiring might not be costly but the plumbing will add up to a pretty penny. A lavatory, a sink in the treatment room, water laid on in the ward, or whatever you call it.

"It's lucky they brought the town water out here, so you folks have plenty. I remember when this was a real farm, and all they had was one dug well. That's how old I am, seventy-five exactly, and I remember when this was called the Spicer place."

He rambled on, and Jenny was thinking, He's just too old. Why did Dad invite him to bid? "Mr. Caulfield, can't you give us a rough idea of the cost?" she asked impatiently.

"No, I can't, young lady," he said. "I have to go home and take my graph paper and draw your daddy some sketches. It's got to look artistic; it can't look like somebody said, 'Hell, here's some useless space, we'll make an animal hospital out of it.' Then I'll sit down with my yellow pad and figure out how much the job will approximately cost. Folks I've worked for will tell you I stick pretty close to my estimates."

"Mr. Steen is doing the same thing," Dr. Wren told Jenny. "He promised us a figure tomorrow morning."

"Mark Steen has some so-called experts to help him there at Howard Lumber," Mr. Caulfield said. "I do the whole thing in my own head. I'll be here at nine next Sunday with my estimates."

He stalked away, backed, and turned his dirty car.

43

He swung too wide and almost hit the Wrens' mail-box, and charged into the line of traffic. Brakes shrieked and drivers yelled. The Wrens watched his departure and Jenny said, "Daddy, I can't see why you asked him to put in a bid. He's just too old."

"Jen, you've seen the remodeling of the Historical Society on Main Street. It's beautiful, and Eben did that."

"He's too old," she repeated stubbornly.

"Age has nothing to do with anything. Is Dr. Everts too old to practice veterinary medicine? You'd be the first to fire up if anyone suggested that, but your Uncle Jim is pushing seventy-six." That shut Jenny up.

"We'll see what the two of them come up with," Dr. Tom said. "Then we'll decide."

6

Dr. Everts paid them a formal call that same afternoon. He arrived at four, yelling, "Sun's over the yard arm!"

He was well-groomed as always, white shirt gleaming, thick, silver hair shining, his cheeks rosy as a girl's. His suit and topcoat however were covered with dog hair. Jenny shook out the black topcoat. "You should have bought tweed," she scolded. "Then people couldn't tell you keep red setters!"

The bag he produced contained a thermos of whiskey sours, an iced Coke for Jenny, crackers, cheese, and herring in cream. They gathered around the kitchen table for this feast.

Old Doc was bubbling over about a case; he and the Wrens adored shoptalk. This time it was a German shepherd–collie mix that had developed cataracts. The owner was ready to spend any amount to have his dog's sight partially restored. Old Doc had inveigled an eye doctor at Moss City Hospital into doing the operation. He was young and earnest, and eager to develop his surgical skills. He was only afraid that his fellow doctors might learn that he was operating on animals for free. Jenny's father jumped at the invitation to assist at the operation.

45

Having dispensed drinks and good cheer, Dr. Everts prepared to leave. Jenny brushed his coat and helped him into it. At the door he delivered his ultimatum. "By the way," he said, "I'm underwriting you, Tom. Setting you up in business. It'll be a loan. If you renege on the payments I'll have the sheriff at your door so fast it'll make your head swim!"

"You're doing nothing of the kind," Dr. Wren told him.

Old Doc called back from the darkness, "Oh yes, I am. See if I don't!"

"We can't take your money!" Jenny shouted.

"We can't take his money," she repeated after Dr. Jim was gone.

"No, not under any circumstances," her father agreed. "We're already indebted for a lifetime of kindness."

On Sunday morning Mr. Steen came as he had promised, but he brought the news that he couldn't take on the job. His boss had contracted to build several houses in a new development, so the Wren job would have to wait. Dr. Wren asked how long and Mr. Steen said, "Six months."

"I can't wait," Dr. Wren said. "I have to start earning a living."

"You'd do well to hire Eben," Mr. Steen told him. "Nobody in town can give you a better job."

They lived in a kind of limbo that following week, waiting for Mr. Caulfield's report. School-wise, it was a bad week for Jenny. She fouled up on a book report and daydreamed in a chemistry test and got a C. Her mind was on what was happening at home. Her father too was acting like a ship that had lost its rudder. His life was built around his practice and now he had no practice except for house calls.

On Sunday morning Dr. Wren kept consulting his watch. "I hope Eben's prompt," he fretted. "That eye surgeon is coming to Old Doc's at eleven, and I can't miss that."

Good as his word, right at nine o'clock the contractor charged into the yard. No wonder the fenders of his car were pleated; he used it like a battering ram. "I've got it. We're all set," he announced, and marched into the kitchen. Jenny cleared the table so he could spread out the sheets.

She had to admit the sketches were good. He had given the waiting room a big door framed by wrought-iron work. The two levels of the roof line made the addition artistic, as Mr. Caulfield pointed out. He had allowed two feet for a garden border between the building and the macadam drive and had drawn in some fancy planting.

Jenny asked why they needed the elegant wrought iron. "To look nice," Mr. Caulfield told her. "You can grow clematis on it. Blue clematis, that looks lovely on white clapboard."

"Isn't wrought iron expensive?" she asked.

"It costs, yes. But we have to throw in a few nice touches."

"What's the weathervane doing on the kennel end?"

"It's telling what way the wind's blowing." The

contractor was beginning to sound huffy.

"I always wet my finger and stick it up to find out which way the wind's blowing," Jenny told him. Then she felt her father's foot on hers, warning her, and added, "But it looks lovely."

"She wants to know what weathervanes cost," Mr. Caulfield said. "In the neighborhood of ninety dollars, young lady. I'll tell you what. If I bring the job in close to my estimates, then you can afford it, but if the job runs over, then I'll pay for it. Howsomever, a gilded weathervane of a running horse is going to be sitting on top of that roof!"

He circled a figure at the bottom of a long column. "That's what the job comes to."

Twelve thousand, five hundred was a lot better than thirty thousand. Jenny nodded agreement when her father said, "That doesn't seem too far out of line."

The doctor left then to keep his date with Dr. Everts. Jenny offered Mr. Caulfield coffee, and he said no; he'd like tea. People drank too much coffee. He looked around and admired the Haviland china and the pewter on the pine sideboard.

He mentioned that the Howard Lumber Company wanted to hire him as a foreman. "I could be building those new houses on Hemlock Ridge," he bragged. "I hate building cheap, though. I'd rather take this job and give your daddy an honest piece of work."

He noisily drank his tea, then pulled on his wool mackinaw. He stopped by the sideboard and took down a silver bowl, upended it, and studied it. Jenny had always vaguely understood there was something special about this piece. "Where'd it come from?" he asked.

"It came down in my father's family."

"How long have they lived in these parts?"

"Since before the Revolution, I guess."

"Did it ever occur to anybody this could be a genuine Paul Revere, the feller who blew the whistle on the British?"

Jenny was startled but didn't show it. Her feeling was growing that she and this old man were never going to be bosom pals. "I doubt that's so," she said.

"You an expert on silver?"

"No, but I'd know if it was a genuine Paul Revere."

"Then you're an expert."

"No, I am not!"

"Somebody who is one ought to look at it," Mr. Caulfield said. "If it's an original, then it belongs in a museum, not in a kitchen where thieves can break in and steal."

He went out. Some cats were sunning on the stone step; he petted one and set it out of the way to make room for his feet.

Twelve thousand, five hundred dollars, Jenny was thinking. Actually she felt like dancing. The insurance would reduce that to only two thousand, five hundred.

Not that they were in the clear, though. They had to eat while the ell was being renovated. Light bills and oil bills and water bills would come due. And by hook or by crook they had to pay off the old debt for Martha's illness. And the new hospital had to be furnished, and that meant a lot of expensive operating room equipment. How much would all that come to?

She busied herself fixing a hearty lunch. Earlier in the week Mrs. Randall had brought them a baked ham because she was afraid they would starve, now that she didn't cook their dinners. Jenny cubed what was left, and made cheese and macaroni, stirring in the ham. Then she fixed a salad and waited for her father.

"How's the dog?" was her first question when he came in.

"We can't tell until the bandages are off," he told her. "Then we'll know by his actions whether he can see. It was beautiful watching that young man work."

Jenny poured tea and when the doctor looked at her inquiringly, she said, "People drink too much coffee."

"Bossy, bossy," he said, but when he had fixed his he admitted, "This is all right. There's one thing about tea: it picks you up but it doesn't slam you down."

Jenny was waiting. "Well?" she said.

"What do you think?"

"I think it sounds great. The estimate, I mean. Of course we lose the garage, and your car will be left out in the weather. We'll have to come up with eating money, and pay the interest on what we owe the bank, and pay the monthly bills. But we won't borrow more money from the bank because we'll use my college account."

"No," he said. "We won't touch a cent of that."

"Dad, it's the best way."

"No. Only over my dead body!"

With that they were off and running. He asked how long she had been entertaining that idea and she said, "Since the morning after the fire."

"I wouldn't touch your money with a ten-foot pole!"

"How about a five-foot pole?" she asked.

That made him laugh, and when he caught himself laughing that made him mad all over again. In the midst of the argument the telephone rang. Somebody's cat was constipated. He said, "Madam, give your constipated damned cat a tablespoon of mineral oil and leave me in peace; today's Sunday and my day of rest!" Of course he had to call the woman back and apologize.

"Who was that?" Jenny asked.

"Mrs. Little."

"The little widow woman," Jenny said. "The one who wants to marry you. That makes two."

"What do you mean, two?"

"There's Miss Eve Simmons."

"Get off my back!" Dr. Wren snarled.

The telephone rang again and it was Thursa. "Can I come over?"

"No!" Jenny shouted. "My father and I are having a fight!"

She had just sat down when the phone rang for the third time. "Put your daddy on," Mr. Caulfield ordered. "You listen too."

Jenny took the hall phone. Mr. Caulfield explained that he had just come home from Sunday lunch with his wife's family. "And there I ran into a piece of bad news," he said. "People at the lunch were talking about your fire. I allowed as how I had the job sewed up, to turn the ell into a hospital.

"My wife's nephew spoke up. He's on the Zoning Board, and he said, 'Oh no, you're not.' It seems there's a zoning law against including humans and animals under the same roof, in a business enterprise, a pet shop, or a breeding kennel, or a veterinary hospital. You're zoned in a residential area, and it's lucky you had the hospital on the property before the town voted for zoning. My wife's nephew says you can rebuild on the same spot, to the same size, twenty-six by forty feet."

"At a cost of thirty thousand," Dr. Wren said.

"At a cost of thirty thousand," Mr. Caulfield agreed. "I guess you and your daughter will have to sit down and do some more thinking. When you decide you can give me a call."

The Wrens were in a very sober mood indeed when they returned to the table. "Daddy, now you're going to have to use my money," Jenny said. "It's just sitting there in the bank. If we had to borrow the whole amount we'd have to pull against an awful debt because the interest rates are out of sight."

"When did you get to be an expert on finance?" he asked.

"I had a talk with Hokie Jones. And don't try to put me down."

"I'm not putting you down."

"I think you are, Daddy. If I were your son, sitting here, and we were talking about our hospital where we'd both practice, you'd sound different."

"Jen, you're wrong!"

She said no more. Ever since she was a small child, though, she had wondered if her father wasn't disappointed that his only child had turned out to be a girl. He would never admit it. But wouldn't any father feel that way?

"I'm sorry," Dr. Wren said. "Maybe it did sound as though I was trying to put you down. The fact is, I'm paralyzed by the mere thought of touching your college account. It means a lot to me that someday you'll hang out your shingle in the front yard."

They quieted down. Truth had been spoken, and they felt like friends again. They agreed that what they needed was financial advice. Dr. Wren had plenty of pals at the bank, and he decided to talk to William Hill, the vice-president.

"How will we live in the meantime?" The doctor sounded gloomy.

Jenny was surprised. Apparently this question had just occurred to him. "How much does it cost to run this place every month?" she asked. "Food, water, electricity?"

"Telephone, garbage removal, taxes, insurance, to name a few more. Bills come in from all directions on the first of the month."

Jenny repeated her question, "How much does it cost to run this place?"

"I don't know."

Jenny told herself, Don't get pushy again. She said carefully, "Dad, what do you mean, you don't know?"

"I just pay the bills as best I can."

Jenny let that statement lie there. Had they always lived this way, hand to mouth? she wondered.

He sensed her silent criticism. He got up, announcing, "I've got a date; I'm supposed to pick up Eve at five." He sounded as though he was daring Jenny to knock a chip off his shoulder.

He came down looking spruce, and she said, "So long," and morosely watched him go.

Actually she was longing for another female to talk to. Advice, that was what she needed. She thought of Thursa, but Thursa would only blindly agree with whatever Jenny said. She thought of Mrs. Osborne, next door, but decided against that. Any talk with an older person usually turned into a hassle.

Who else? The only name she came up with was Sara Harrison.

The Harrisons were New Yorkers who had settled in Harley. Sara was an oddball, a real brain. Her whole family was very intelligent. With Hokie Jones and Jenny herself, Sara belonged to a triumvirate of the three brightest students, if a dumb school like Harley High could claim it had any really bright students.

Jenny had always been drawn to Sara. Their friendship was a tentative sort of thing. Several times Sara had mentioned in an offhand way that she would like to have Jenny come out to the Harrisons' farm. The visit hadn't materialized, but the friendship had continued.

Did Jenny really want to corner a casual friend like Sara, though, and try to have a heart-to-heart talk? No, she decided.

54

A big batch of homework needed her attention, but the mere thought was revolting. She wandered through the house and vaguely noticed that it was untidy and there were dust kittens under chairs. She glanced in a mirror and vaguely realized that her hair looked greasy.

She washed it, then prowled the house again, a towel around her shoulders, thinking, I've got to talk to some human being. How about this thing, Dad and Miss Simmons? I don't want to start making a mountain out of a molehill — .

The telephone rang. "Jen, if I bring Miss Horowitz's cat over, could your dad take out the stitches?" Hokie asked. "He spayed it a few days before the fire."

Jenny was so tired of her lonesome brooding she sounded very enthusiastic. "Great, Hoke! Dad's not here, but you and I can do it."

She changed from worn jeans into new red pants and a white blouse. Why she changed she didn't know, because Hokie was used to seeing her at her worst.

He brought the calico in a carrier. She was wailing plaintively, and when Jenny opened the carrier she scuttled around the kitchen. That only lasted a few minutes. She got her confidence back and emerged from a corner to be petted.

Hokie seemed nervous. "What's the matter?" Jenny asked. "Didn't you ever take out stitches before?"

"No. Have you?"

"Sure, lots of times. I've held so many animals for Dad, I get bored, so sometimes we switch off, and he holds while I clip."

"It sounds like practicing medicine without a license," Hokie said doubtfully.

"Sometimes a cat takes out her own stitches," Jenny told him. "There certainly isn't any law that says a cat can't take out her own stitches."

Jenny fetched her father's medical bag. Hokie sat with the cat on his knees, belly up. He had a way with animals and could practically hypnotize them instantly. He stroked the calico and murmured to her and she relaxed and purred.

Jenny snipped the stitches near the knots, tested gently with tweezers to make sure the thread was ready to slip out, and pulled. The cat didn't even jump; it just kept on purring. Jenny washed the area with antiseptic, and the job was done.

Hokie didn't seem in any hurry to leave, but held the calico, scratching its ears. His face reddened because he had something to say. "Jen, your hair looks nice that way," he blurted.

This was the first personal remark Hokie had ever addressed to her. Jenny had forgotten her hair was still loose, she had been so interested in the minor operation they were performing. She tossed it back, realizing that maybe it wasn't so bad, being a girl and having a lot of nice hair to toss around. "I'd better go and braid it," she said.

"You don't have to do that just on account of me," Hokie said gallantly.

7

Jenny was used to dealing with a Hokie Jones who was poised for instant flight. This one sat contentedly, sheltering the calico cat in his arms. Jenny's mother had always offered hospitality to anybody who came into her kitchen, so of course Jenny did the same. "How about a cup of coffee?" she offered.

"No, I don't think so."

"How about soda?"

"No, but if you have a little milk you can spare — "

She poured a glass of milk and set a plate of cookies on the table. After that they sat and nodded at each other like a pair of idiots. Finally Hokie said loudly, "How are you coming on that last chemistry experiment?"

"Oh, that," Jenny said. "I'm not. I asked Sara Harrison to do my half." Sara and Jenny were chem lab partners.

"Jen, you can't do that!"

"Well, I did it," Jenny said indifferently. Problems here at home were so overwhelming, school problems didn't seem worth thinking about.

Hoke made the effort and launched another topic of conversation. "How about the hospital?"

"I haven't had a chance to tell you," Jenny said.

"Using the ells is out, on account of some stupid zoning law. We'll have to rebuild in the yard."

Hoke had rather a small head on top of his long body, and you could almost see the wheels buzzing inside it. "That will come roughly to thirty-one thousand," he said.

She had watched him doing lightning calculations in math at school, so she wasn't surprised, but she asked, "How did you come up with that figure?"

"The old hospital was twenty-six feet by forty. I paced it off once when I was trying to visualize what kind of a hospital I would have, if I went into vet medicine instead of regular medicine. Thirty dollars a square foot is the going rate these days. So that comes to thirty-one, two hundred."

"That's about right," she told him. "Mr. Caulfield cut it to thirty."

"Are you going ahead?"

She hesitated, and that gave Hokie the idea he was overstepping the bounds. He said, "Excuse me, I shouldn't pry," and shot to his feet and grabbed his jacket.

"No, wait, Hokie," Jenny protested. "You weren't prying. I was just thinking out my answer."

"I'll see you," he said, and bounded out the door. Annoyed, she watched him lope away, thinking, Anybody that thin-skinned is a bloody nuisance to have around.

During the next few days Jenny and her father were so uptight they didn't communicate much. He hired somebody to remove the debris. A front-end loader came and scooped it up and a truck took it away. Hokie had piled the cages to one side, hoping they might be salvageable. When the Wrens looked out now, the yard was level and bare, but they didn't mention this.

Dr. Wren broke down first. "I can't stand this cat and dog existence," he said. "You're sore because I've left you alone a few evenings."

"I don't think dogs and cats have such a bad time of it," she said. "Not ours, anyway. And no, I'm not sore on that account."

"Yes, you are."

"Okay, yes I am," she said, and snapped off the TV, hoping they were going to have a real donnybrook.

"No, you're not sore," he said, and gave her his one-sided grin. She couldn't help it, she laughed, and the tension was eased. "When are you going to call Mr. Caulfield?" she asked.

"Do you think we should go ahead?"

She noted the "we." Aha! she thought, he included me. "I don't see that we have much choice," she told him.

"It's the amount that scares me. We'll also have to borrow money to live on. Eating's getting kind of slim around here."

"We'll use my college account and save the awful interest rates," Jenny stated.

He didn't argue that issue any more. "That will save us from taking out a new mortgage," he agreed. "Your mother and I worked awfully hard to pay off the first one. Thanks, honey, for the wonderful offer. I'll start putting your money back in the bank as soon as I start earning again."

On Sunday night winter took a late slap at the northeast and dropped six inches of snow. It stopped before daylight. Worthless took one look when Jenny let him out on Monday morning, and headed back in. She had to push him out to do his necessaries.

Dr. Wren appeared, and he looked vague. "What am I supposed to do with myself all day?" he asked helplessly. "I'll clear the drive, but after that what am I going to do?"

"You've got to make your mind up," Jenny told him. "Mr. Caulfield has to have a yes or a no, or else he'll take on another job and we'll really be out in the cold. Why don't you call him today and say yes? And today you could see the people at the bank. We've got the ten thousand from the insurance and the nine thousand from my college money, so the bank will have to come across with the rest."

He opened his mouth, then closed it. "What were you going to say?" she challenged him.

"Just that you seem to have taken over."

"Somebody has to get this show on the road," she told him.

Thursa as usual had saved a seat for Jenny on the bus. She chattered steadily; she saved up her remarks all weekend and poured them out to Jenny on Monday mornings. Jenny just said, "Uh-huh," and went on pondering her problems. Like, was there enough money in the checking account to pay last month's bills? Was she going to have to keep pressuring her father? Would he just dawdle along, or would he take the initiative? Her future was tied so tightly with his, she had a right to be bossy.

What if Miss Eve Simmons came charging into the picture and that romance really heated up? How would that affect Jenny's future?

She tried hard to apply herself to math and World History II in her first two periods. She found it hard these days to really connect with her school work. She had study hall at eleven this Monday; it alternated with phys. ed. Her study hall was in the library, and it coincided with Hokie's.

The librarian was a sensible woman who recognized that Hokie and Jenny were so bright they didn't need to study, and she made no objection when Hokie drew his chair close to Jenny's. As long as they kept their voices down, she would leave them alone. "Jen, I've got two tickets for the Theater League next Saturday night," Hokie began.

This, Jenny knew, was a group which had bought the Grange Hall on the state road, where they put on plays. She had little interest in the theater. Formerly she might have said, "So what?" This was a new Hokie, though, who was making tentative advances, like admiring her hair. She didn't feel like slapping him down, so she said, "Oh?"

"We're putting on *Le Médecin malgré lui.*"

"What's that?"

"Molière's play. We read it last year in French II."

"Oh, no!" Jenny exclaimed, startled that anybody would suggest she go to see anything so deadly dull.

Her "Oh, no!" came out very loud. Jenny smiled at the librarian, apologizing. Hokie, too shy to cope with any rebuff, bent over his books, his ears flaming. "Is it in French?" Jenny whispered.

"No, it's in English, but if you don't want to go, that's all right."

"You've bought the tickets?"

"No, they were free. I work with the Theater League."

"You ACT?"

"No, I help with the business end, and properties, stuff like that."

"Okay, I'd like to go. And thanks." Jenny thought to herself, Hey, I've got a date for Saturday night, even if it's only with Hokie Jones.

During that week, Jenny and her father still weren't communicating too well. He didn't keep her informed of his financial negotiations, he simply announced the result. "By the way," he mentioned, one night, "the bank's willing to lend me the money. On my own recognizance."

"That means we don't have to put up any security?"

"Right. It seems I have a better reputation around the town as a businessman that I do in my own house."

She let that pass, and she also let pass his using "I" when she was using "we." "What's the interest rate?" she asked.

"Nine percent."

"That's terrible."

"It's the going rate, and I have no choice. Eben's

63

starting tomorrow if it's a fair day. He has to give the concrete slab a skim coat of fresh cement to level it."

They talked about the hospital, but Jenny's mind wandered. She had a brand-new, personal problem connected with her coming date. Should she wear a dress in honor of Hokie's invitation? And how about leaving her hair loose, the way Hokie liked it?

On Saturday morning she really tangled with this problem and studied the contents of her closet. It held a lot of pants and shirts, but very few dresses. She wished she could consult with some female who was clothes-smart because she herself was just plain clothes-dumb. She picked out a gold color dress she liked. Unfortunately the hem sagged.

Mrs. Osborne had been trying to mother her ever since her own mother died, but Jenny had resisted because she and her father were so self-sufficient. Now she thought, I'll give her a chance to do her thing. With the dress over her arm, she crossed the yard.

Mrs. Osborne was at the stove stirring something that smelled wonderful. She greeted Jenny with little cries of delight, snatched the dress, and fetched her sewing basket. Jenny asked what the smell was and Mrs. Osborne said it was beef stew. "Old Doc adores that," Jenny told her. "Could you give me the recipe?" Mrs. Osborne handed her a pencil and pad and went on with the hemming.

"I'd love to have you and your father come for supper with us tonight," Mrs. Osborne said.

64

"Thanks very much, but I have a date," Jenny told her. "I suppose Dad does, too."

"I've noticed that your father's been going out, lately," Mrs. Osborne said.

"It's with that Eve Simmons, who teaches at the middle school."

"Yes, I've heard. She's a lovely woman. Our Nicky has her for English."

Jenny hesitated. Then she burst out, "I don't know that I think it's so great!"

"Why, Jenny?"

"Mom's only been dead two years!"

There. She had said it. Jenny's eyes filled with tears. Mrs. Osborne pushed a box of tissues over to her and waited until Jenny had control of herself. Then Mrs. Osborne said gently, "I know, dear, it's hard for you to accept the fact that your father would ever put another woman in your mother's place. I loved your mother; she was my closest friend. But Jenny dear, life is for the living. That's a harsh fact, but it's true. We have to pick up and go on. And I love your father too and I'd like to see him happy. I can't help but be glad that he's found a companion."

"Dad and I are pals. Or at least we used to be!" Jenny cried.

"Of course you are! It's wonderful, the relationship you have with your father. But it's not the same thing."

They said no more. Jenny glumly watched her finish the hem. "It's a lovely dress and I hope you have a lovely time on your date, dear," Mrs. Osborne said. Jenny thanked her and went home.

Maybe the older woman was right, Jenny thought. She was willing to bet that the rest of Dr. Tom's friends would agree with Mrs. Osborne. But everything was changed and everything would be different, forever after. And not for the better, Jenny thought. Oh, no. Not by a long shot!

8

The truck from Howard's came that afternoon to deliver the first load of lumber, and Eben Caulfield arrived to direct how he wanted it piled. He was all over the place, getting in the delivery man's way, and once the burly driver had to pick him up bodily and set him to one side. Jenny came out to watch, and thought, He hops around like a silly sparrow.

"Where's your pa?" he asked after the truck had gone.

"He had a call to go out." Jenny said.

"Will you tell him that if tomorrow dawns fair I aim to start the framing?"

"Tomorrow's Sunday," she pointed out.

"Nobody knows better than I do it's Sunday. That's the day I spend in the bosom of my wife's family. Now I've got an excuse to avoid those family gatherings because your Pa needs me. So will you tell him?"

His small, intelligent eyes bored into Jenny's, and they twinkled; it occurred to her that whether she liked him or not, he apparently liked her. "Okay, Mr. Caulfield, I'll tell him," she said. "I hope tomorrow dawns fair." He bounded into his pickup and off he went.

There wasn't any dinner to fix in the Wren house that evening. The doctor came downstairs looking really neat in a blue blazer with brass buttons. He mentioned that he wished Jenny would join him and Eve. This time she could tell him, "No thanks, Daddy. I have a date."

His eyebrows shot toward his receding hairline. This was a startling turn of events. Jenny's dates were few and far between. "Who with?" he asked.

"Hokie. He's taking me to the theater."

"The movies?"

"No, the Creative Arts Theater."

Her father's eyebrows climbed even higher. "You're going to soak up some culture."

"That's what I aim to do, soak up some culture," she agreed.

"Well, honey, I hope you have a real good time," he said. "Do you need any mad money?"

"What's that?"

"I forgot that we have a generation gap here," he said. "In the olden days a girl carried some cash so she'd have a way to get home in case she had a fight with her boy friend."

"I doubt any girl has to be afraid of that if her date's with Hokie Jones," Jenny told him.

Her father insisted that she take the five dollars anyway. She said she wasn't carrying a purse, and he said she could tuck it inside her bra. "Dad, this is absolutely ridiculous," she protested, but took the money to please him.

She had a great time on her date, she really did.

The Creative Arts people had turned the Grange Hall into a nice little theater. The play seemed dated and quaint, but it wasn't too dull and the cast was wonderful. They really threw themselves into the spirit of the thing.

When the performance was over and the audience had gone, the Arts group went downstairs for a late supper. The basement had been converted into a lounge with tables and comfortable chairs. Hot and cold food were served buffet-style.

Jenny was surprised by the attitude of these adults toward Hokie. Clearly they were very fond of him; they kidded him but there wasn't any sting in it. Jenny thought how astonished the high-school kids would be if they could see this Hokie Jones. He didn't seem so plain tonight, so funny-looking. His face was flushed and he laughed a lot. No, he wasn't the same boy who scuttled around the corridors at school.

He brought plates of food and sat with Jenny, parrying the jokes, answering back with some funny quips of his own. It dawned on Jenny that she was getting a lot of attention solely because she was Hokie's date.

He took her home at midnight. "How about coming in and having a Coke or something?" she suggested.

"I'd better not," he said. "My folks get up tight if I'm out late."

"Well," she said. They just stood there, they were both awkward about this dating business. "Hokie, I had a really great time," she told him.

"Would you go again?"

"I'd love to go again."

"Do you mean it?"

"I mean it," she said. "Good night, Hoke, see you around." He hadn't made a pass, although he certainly had the opportunity.

Sunday dawned fair, as Mr. Caulfield had hoped. He arrived early with a hammer stuck in the pocket of his raggedy pants, and began nailing two-by-fours, starting the framing. It occurred to Jenny the word was "ferocious"; he ferociously pounded nails. Her father worked along with him, hauling two-by-fours and holding them as the boss carpenter directed. After awhile Dr. Wren started to wilt, and Eben jeered that this was probably the first honest work the doctor had ever done.

At noon Jenny went out with sandwiches and drinks. By late afternoon the skeleton framework of the new hospital was up. Mr. Caulfield didn't seem in the least weary when he left. Dr. Wren, dog-tired, looked to Jenny for comfort. "We'll have our new hospital before too long," he said.

She agreed, noting the "we."

Her father put his arm around her. "Honey, I've been thinking," he said. "You know Eve Simmons."

"I don't know her, but I know who she is."

"I think it would be a great idea if we asked her to the house. Weekends are going to be hectic around here because I'll be working with Eben. But next week's your school vacation week, and we could have her then."

"For dinner?"

"Oh no, that would be too much to ask you to manage. How about tea?"

"I never put on a tea party in my life," Jenny said. "Mom used to invite ladies for tea, though, so I have an idea how it's done."

A cloud crossed his face at Jenny's mention of her mother. "I'm sure you'll do it nicely, Jenny," he said. "Will Tuesday be all right?"

"Tuesday's fine."

There wasn't much to putting on a tea party, and yet Jenny managed to make a very big deal out of it. On Monday she asked Thursa to come and help her clean. In return, Jenny offered to help whip into shape an English paper which was giving Thursa an awful tussle.

Thursa leaped at the chance when Jenny explained the reasons behind this sudden desire for cleanliness. Her round, fair face lit up like a light bulb and she cried, "Oh, that's lovely! I adored Miss Simmons when I had her for a teacher, and you'll be crazy about her too when you get to know her."

"I doubt I'll ever adore her if I know her for a thousand years," Jenny said.

Thursa ignored that and took a quick tour through the rooms. "Leave it to me," she told Jenny. "I'll soon have this place looking great."

Jenny settled down at the kitchen table with Thursa's jumbled notes, and began putting them into neat order. All she saw of her friend was Thursa's fat bottom straining the seams of her jeans as she fiercely attacked the dirt. Worthless ran wild-eyed from room to room, trying to keep out of the way.

Jenny had a vague picture in her mind of those pleasant occasions when her mother had entertained friends. She chose three Haviland cups, saucers, and dessert plates that had no nicks. She polished teaspoons. For a long time she stared at the silver tea set on a top shelf. Finally she decided, I might as well go the whole hog, and took it down and started cleaning it.

Dr. Wren seemed very appreciative of the efforts that were being made. Jenny gave him his marching orders; she needed lemons, a loaf of thin-cut bread, and a roll of prepared cookie dough. He asked if she wanted a fire in the fireplace and she said Yes, because that was part of the picture of her mother's parties.

When Thursa finished, the downstairs was immaculate. She mourned because she had no flowers for a tasteful arrangement to dress up the tea table. She asked if she could come next day and make the tea and serve. Jenny told her she was to stay away. Jenny would give her a full account of the bloody affair after it was over.

"Jen, when you know her better you'll love her," Thursa insisted as she departed. Jenny wondered, Was Thursa as innocent as she seemed to be? Couldn't she see what it would do to Jenny's life if the Simmons woman moved in and took over?

The silver teapot, sugar bowl, creamer, and tray were coming along nicely. Dr. Wren came in at dinner time, and Jenny was still working on it. After they had eaten they moved to the living room to watch the news, but Jenny excused herself, "I have to finish a job."

He wandered out when the news ended. She was scrubbing the teapot's raised design with a toothbrush and silver polish. "What are you doing, hon?" he asked.

"I'm polishing my mother's tea set," Jenny said. "It's a shame and a disgrace I let my mother's tea set get into such a terrible condition."

He got the message, all right. He went upstairs, and she didn't see him again all evening.

Had she gone too far? Yes, Jenny decided. She had hurt her father deliberately. She had no right to question the depth and strength of his love for her lost mother.

The only way she could make up to him was to be nice to his friend. Jenny took a one-hundred-eighty-degree turn and decided, I'll try to make Miss Simmons's visit a success and not a disaster.

So, the awful tea party didn't turn out to be awful after all.

Eve arrived at four. Jenny gave her a real friendly smile of welcome. The fire the doctor had laid in the living room didn't burn well, and that gave the women something to talk about as they watched his struggles to get it going. Then he brought in the heavy tray and set it on the low table in front of Jenny.

She had watched her mother serve tea and imitated her. "Milk or lemon?" she asked, after she had filled

Miss Simmons's cup. "Daddy, will you pass the bread and butter, please?"

He fell all over himself in his eagerness to make the party go well. He extravagantly praised the thin bread and butter sandwiches and the cookies. Jenny grinned to herself, thinking that what he really needed in his own tea was a slug of rum to buck him up.

Eve carried the conversation easily while Jenny observed her. Jenny herself was looking okay in the gold dress. Miss Simmons, though, looked absolutely marvelous in a pants suit of country tweed with a turtleneck jersey. Her dark hair was done in a French twist, every hair in place. Her face was serene and beautiful.

They talked about Jenny's school career, and about Worthless, who was basking in the fire's glow. They got onto town affairs, and the town's concert series, of which Miss Simmons was chairwoman. The last concert was to take place soon, and Dr. Wren allowed as how he was looking forward to it. "To hear a violinist?" Jenny wanted to snort. "You'll die; you hate fiddles!" She didn't, she just gave her father a wicked glance to let him know she knew he was putting on an act.

Everything Miss Simmons did and said was graceful, and at five she gracefully stood up and thanked Jenny, praised the tea, and left.

What did Dr. Wren expect? That Jenny would cry, "She's beautiful; she's wonderful; she'll make me a dandy stepmother?" Jenny said nothing. He was quiet and thoughtful while he helped carry the tea things to the kitchen. He said, "Thank you, Jenny, for making such a nice little party," and that was all that was said.

Jenny washed the Haviland china and put it away, and wrapped the silver pieces in plastic before she put them back on the top shelf. She didn't plan to polish them again if her father got an urge to invite his friend back for more tea. The episode was over.

9

Jenny was still wishing she had somebody to talk to. It couldn't be an adult because how could you talk to anybody over the ripe old age of twenty? She had some worries she longed to share. Worry over money was at the top of the list. Her father's entanglement with Eve Simmons, that came next. And it seemed to her that she and her father were losing their really great relationship. That came third.

How about Sara Harrison? Sara was so cool and confident and remote, Jenny hesitated to try to push their friendship. Then there was Thursa, who truly loved her, and Jenny loved Thursa back. Thursa was likely to panic, though, if you tried to involve her in a deep discussion.

How about Hokie? Jenny shied away from that. Hokie would bring the conversation around to a stern warning that her schoolwork was slipping. The truth was that she just couldn't seem to connect, and her grades were beginning to show this.

How about Old Doc? Uncle Jim wasn't just an adult, he was an old, old man, and yet Jenny and he had always been able to communicate.

She made the stew from Mrs. Osborne's recipe and it turned out delicious. She made a double amount, so she would have a decent meal for her father if he stayed home for dinner that week. Not that he went out every night; it just seemed that way.

Hokie Jones was working in the yard that day, one of those sunny April days when green was creeping up out of the brown earth. Hokie was straightening the cages he had retrieved from the fire, preparing to spray-paint them. Mr. Caulfield was nailing wood siding to the upright two-by-fours and having a glorious time barking orders at Jenny's father. Dr. Wren looked harassed, but he stuck around because his help saved the expense of an assistant carpenter.

Jenny left this jolly crew and drove to Old Doc's house, the hot stew in an aluminum container beside her on the seat.

The Everts place on North Street had always been Harley's showplace, a big white house with white columns, set in park-like grounds. The grounds weren't kept up the way they used to be and the house needed paint, but nevertheless Jenny felt a thrill as she turned into the drive. She went around to the back where Dr. Everts's hospital occupied the old carriage shed. His car was there, but he wasn't, so she knocked on the back door, calling, "Uncle Jim!" She got no answer and walked in.

The kitchen was messy. Old Doc had no proper help. After his wife died, Jenny's Aunt May, a couple had lived in and taken care of the place. Then they left, and nowadays he got along with day help, a woman to clean, another to cook his meals.

Jenny started through the house, calling, "Hey,

Uncle Jim!" She paused, looking about her. Harley people still called this the drawing room, a spacious room with high windows, Oriental rugs, massive furniture. Shabby it might be, but it was still the grandest room in town. Jenny reached the hall stairs, which swept upward in a semi-circle, and yelled, "If you're up there, answer me!"

She heard him cough. He shuffled to the top of the stairs in his soft slippers and stared down at her, flanked on either side by his red setters. "I'm glad it's you," he said. "Why aren't you in school?"

"We have a week's vacation. I've brought your lunch. Come and eat it while it's hot."

She began tidying the kitchen. He tasted the stew, pronounced it magnificent, added a large dollop of bourbon and ate the whole thing while she sat and watched him. "I needed that," he said, and burped. "Baby, you're a living doll." He was truly a gentleman of the old school but sometimes he put on this act.

He poured a glass of soda for her and made a bourbon highball for himself. This was something that secretly scared Jenny, and she said carefully, "Uncle Jim, isn't it kind of early for a drink? Sometimes I wonder if you're not getting to be a wee bit of an alcoholic."

"It's nice of you to worry, dearie, but I'm not," he said. "If I ever suspect I'm turning into a fall-down drunk, I promise I'll call in the Alcoholics Anonymous boys. How are things going at your place? I don't suppose I'll ever forgive your daddy because he wouldn't let me finance the new hospital."

"You've done too much for us already," she told him.

"Tell your father not to buy a new operating table. I'm giving him my old one. I ordered a new one because I fell foul of a smooth-talking equipment salesman. I need a new table like I need a hole in my head but I'm stuck with it."

She knew this was a lie; the table in his operating room was only two years old, the most efficient and expensive kind. This was Uncle Jim's sneaky way to save her father several hundred dollars.

"I asked you how things are going," he said.

"Pretty well. Eben Caulfield is running Dad ragged but the hospital is going up awfully fast."

His shrewd eyes were studying her face. "How is it with you?"

"Okay."

"Not entirely okay."

"Well, Dad's got this new friend," Jenny began, then stopped, not knowing how far she wanted to go.

"Eve Simmons," he stated. "Teaches English. Fine stock; her folks come from over Blessingham way. Her uncle raised Arabians."

"Arabian whats?"

"Arabian horses. Honey, does it really bug you because your daddy's dating a woman?"

"I don't know," Jenny confessed.

"I'll tell you what. How about going on my calls with me this afternoon? I have to take a run up Long

80

Mountain way. Vladimir Hanson says he has a horse whose foot is all swole up." Jenny nodded. "Thank you for the magnificent lunch," Doc said, and kissed her.

He picked her up at two and they drove out of town and into the hills. Halfway up Long Mountain macadam gave way to dirt road, and Dr. Everts fought the ruts to the top. They emerged from the woods at the crest, and he turned off the ignition. "Take a gander," he ordered.

"I've seen this view before," she told him.

"Did you really see it? How the green is just beginning to creep in? How soft the hills look this time of year? I thought of something. It's a green blush. The land blushes green."

"Uncle Jim, you're a nut," she said.

"Really look," he commanded sternly. "People don't spend enough time really looking."

She did, to please him, and saw more than a pretty view of the town, of church spires and the shimmer of Town Pond, of hills beyond. She saw how solid those hills were, how clear the sky. It crossed her mind, Hokie would have something positive and interesting to say about this. "What did you call it, 'a green blush'?" she said. "Uncle Jim, you're a poet."

He was staring steadily as though he had to fill his mind with this western view. "Spring is covering over the bare bones, but the bare bones are beautiful too," he said.

She didn't answer because she was thinking

deeply. Her old friend was expecting a heart-to-heart talk, but now she realized she didn't really want to get into one. The Eve Simmons problem didn't bug her as much as the money problem. If she even mentioned that, though, Uncle Jim would come down on her like a ton of bricks, insisting on financing the hospital, insisting on financing her future. And that she and her father could not allow. They had to hang onto their independence, work out their problems themselves — .

"Let's have it, Jenny," Dr. Everts broke in on her thoughts.

Reluctantly, she began, "Well, you know how things were planned, Uncle Jim. I was going to be a vet and be partners with Dad. But now I don't know whether that will ever come about. I mean, Dad's got this girl."

"She's not a girl; she's a thirty-year-old woman. Handsome, too."

"Okay. She's beautiful, I'll give her that. But I was going to run the house for Dad. Our names were going to be on the shingle together."

"So what's put an end to that plan?"

Jenny was near to crying. "Uncle Jim, it just seems all wrong! How could he want to put somebody else in my mother's place so soon?"

"It's been two years," Old Doc said. "That's seven hundred nights, seven hundred days. I found out after I lost your Aunt May how long the days and nights can be." He waited. Then he asked, "Do you believe that Martha would want your father to grieve forever?"

"Not forever, maybe. But you never remarried. You never put anybody else in Aunt May's place."

"And I turned into a sour old man. I wouldn't want your father to suffer the same fate. You know, Jenny dear, going through life we only meet up with a few people we really love. I sometimes think of love as little circles. You and your father, for one. Your father and Martha for another. My May and I. I share one with your father too, because I truly love that man. You and I share a circle; you're as dear to me as my own flesh and blood. Now honey, things change. Your mother's gone; and if your Dad finds true love with another woman, he's a lucky man. Some people never find even one person to share with. They go through life unloving and unloved."

Old Doc stopped, but Jenny offered no comment. "We'd better get this show on the road," he said, and drove on.

He turned through broken gates into a hard-packed yard and stopped by a sagging barn. A man emerged, called, "Glad to see you, Doc," and went back in.

An overwhelming stink of rotting manure hit Jenny, but she followed Old Doc. It took her a minute to get used to the darkness. The farmer led out a beautiful bay mare and held her head harness. Dr. Everts picked up her front hoof to examine it. "Who does she belong to?" he asked.

"I'm wintering her for a city feller, a Mr. Silvert."

83

"You're doing a lousy job, Vladimir," Dr. Everts said. "It took days for her hoof to get this bad. Something's packed in there."

The mare whinnied and struggled while he dug with a surgical probe around her hoof. Jenny helped hold her, murmuring, "There's a good girl." She wasn't looking when Dr. Everts said, "It's out." He filled a large needle, explaining, "Penicillin," and drove the needle into the mare's flank.

He repacked his bag. "Give it hot soaks twice a day," he ordered. "Either Dr. Wren or I will be up this way to look at her next week, and the swelling had better be down. Clean out her stall, and while you're at it, clean out the whole barn. Your own critters deserve a decent place to live."

Hanson evidently knew Old Doc well. He grinned and nodded.

"Your cows been tested?" Dr. Everts demanded.

"Yes, sir. You did it yourself, last fall."

"Did I vaccinate them too?"

"Yes, doc, you did."

The doctor and Jenny got back in the car and descended the mountain. "I'm at the tag end of my spring testing," Dr. Everts explained. "I turned over most of my farm work to your daddy, but I hung onto a few cases. I guess I just like cows. I've got one more herd to do out this way."

"You're testing for tuberculosis?" Jenny asked.

"Yes, and I'll innoculate for brucellosis at the same time. Both diseases can be transmitted to humans."

84

He delivered a lecture on the subject of immunization while he drove along.

The next place was clean; the barns were painted. There were very few successful farms still operating in Harley, and this was one of them. The farmer and two hands were ready to help. The cows were lined up in their stalls inside the big barn, and Dr. Everts passed along behind them, drawing blood from each, injecting it into small vials. Jenny had helped her father with this job, and she numbered the vials to match the numbers on the tags clipped to the cows' ears. When Dr. Everts finished, he passed along the line again, shooting a needleful of the brucellosis vaccine into each animal.

They started home. "You're pretty good help, Jen," Dr. Everts conceded. "You'll make a good vet, even if you are a girl."

She opened her mouth to protest. He added hastily, "I know, I know! If I say anything derogatory to females I'll get the whole Women's Lib down on my neck. I only meant that you can handle the big ones, horses and cows, because you've got a way with animals. It doesn't take brute force; it just takes skill and nerve, and knowing the tricks of the trade. If you don't learn them all at vet college, your pa and I will teach you. We've each got a bagful of tricks."

"It won't be easy to get into a good vet school," Jenny said. "There aren't many. There are so few farms left, vets aren't needed to take care of farm animals. It isn't like it used to be."

"Who says?"

"Hokie Jones says. He looked into it. Lots of kids who can't make it into vet school go into regular medicine as their second choice. Maybe I'll be one of those who don't make it."

"You will."

"Says who?" she demanded.

"Says me," he told her confidently.

10

They were nearing town when Dr. Everts asked, "Do you suppose you could spare me an hour or two of your valuable time? The boy who helps me isn't coming in today."

"Why not?" Jenny said. "My time isn't all that valuable."

The scene in Doc's waiting room was familiar. All the eyes, human and animal, turned to the door when Dr. Everts walked in. Cats howled and dogs on leashes cowered, scared by the strange place and the hospital smell. Jenny followed the doctor into the surgery and he gave her a white coat. "Ask who's first, and take 'em in order," he suggested.

The first patient, a beagle, only needed a distemper innoculation. Jenny held it while Dr. Everts gave the shot, then found the dog's card in the file and made the proper entry. The second patient was a gray cat, brought in for spaying. She'd had food that day, so the doctor couldn't operate until evening when her stomach would be empty. Jenny spread clean newspaper in a cage and set the cat inside.

"Who's next?" she asked.

A weeping woman handed over a white cat. This animal had been emitting howls of pain, and they saw why when Jenny set it on the table. Its face was swollen out of shape. Its owner was so nervous Old Doc sent her back to the waiting room. "Hold him by the scruff of his neck and don't let go," he warned Jenny.

"Aren't you going to anesthetize him?" she asked.

"No. We don't risk that danger unless we have to."

The cat's howls rose several decibels when the doctor started to clip the hair from the swollen cheek. He got a paw free and raked the doctor across the back of the hand. "Stop that, you confounded son of Satan!" Old Doc roared. Jenny had to throw herself across the cat to hold it down.

When the skin was exposed the trouble was plain. "He tangled with another tom and got the worst of the battle," Dr. Everts diagnosed. Jenny saw where the teeth had gone in. Blood and pus poured out of the small holes as the doctor pressed, and she got the full benefit of the foul smell. The cat never stopped yowling and thrashing, and its fright gave it enormous strength.

Dr. Everts pushed the end of a tube of antibiotic ointment inside and worked it around under the loose skin. "Hold on another second, Jen," he ordered. He rapidly shaved a patch on the leg, stuck in the needle, muttering, "Thank God for penicillin." Then to Jenny's astonishment he picked up the cat and kissed it and said, "Good puss."

Jenny put the cat in its mistress's arms, and Dr. Everts came out to speak to her. "You'd better bring him in for neutering," he advised. "I hate to rob him of his manhood, or his cathood, or whatever you want to call it, but if he goes tomcating he's going to get beat up regularly." She agreed she would.

Jenny was about to lead in a dachshund when a commotion erupted outside. A town cop climbed out of his cruiser carrying a small black dog. Its head lolled helplessly over his arm. A young mother and a small boy followed.

Jenny darted ahead to spread clean newspaper on the operating table, and the cop gently laid the dog down. "I hit it," he explained. "It's the kid's pet. I hope it's not broke up too bad."

The doctor's skillful hands were exploring. An enormous respect for him, and her father, and all veterinarians filled Jenny. For human doctors, too. She thought, This is the greatest, to have the skills that stop pain. And give life.

They were all watching Old Doc as if he were God or something. He said, "You stay, Jen, and you too, Officer Breen. The dog has a shattered pelvis and internal injuries."

The mother let out a cry and Jenny hugged her and quickly led her and the child out. When she came back Dr. Everts was getting the needle ready. She thought, I can't stand here and see another one die. Then she realized, I'll see hundreds of them die when I'm a vet. Thousands.

She gathered the dog's head to her breast, softly stroking it. It went heavy in her arms, and she said, "Doc, it's gone."

Tears were pouring down Officer Breen's face.

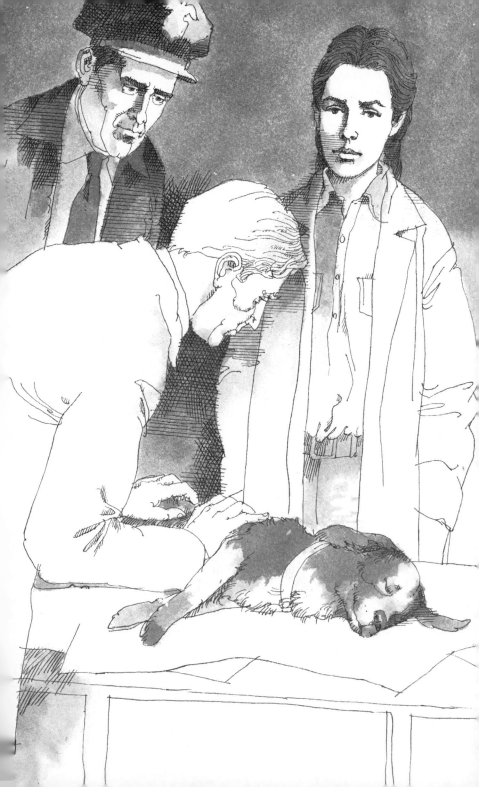

Jenny realized, The kids will never believe it if I tell them I saw a cop cry.

The men carried the broken body to the back room and put it in a plastic bag. The cop asked where he could get the kid another dog, and Dr. Everts suggested he try the town pound where there were always unwanted dogs and puppies. "You'd be doing your boy and some poor mutt a big favor," he told the mother. The little group left.

Patients were still waiting. "How about it, Jen?" Dr. Everts asked. "Have you had enough for the day?"

"I guess not," she said.

He stood back, and she gathered up the blood-soaked papers and sponged off the table. "You can really cut the mustard, Jenny Wren," he commented.

She stayed until the last patient had gone. Uncle Jim offered to drive her home but she said No, she'd walk. "But you're tired," he protested. "We've had a strenuous afternoon."

"Uncle Jim, I just want to be alone."

"So be it," he said. "You're a funny one. Always were and always will be. What do you do when you're alone?"

"I think," she told him. "I never heard that it hurt anybody to do a little thinking now and then."

"There's no point in asking what you think about because you wouldn't tell me," he said.

He was sitting at his desk, putting in his ledger the cases they had handled that afternoon. Jenny noted the neat entries in the small, spidery writing. "I wish

my father could keep a ledger like that!" she exclaimed. "His is a real mess. No wonder he doesn't
know who owes him what!"

"Tom has his faults, but when we add up the score
we're likely to find that the faults add up to mighty
little compared to the virtues," Dr. Everts said.
"Think that one over, child."

She walked down the hill in the twilight, leaving
the quiet streets of the residential area. A pond occupied the center of the town, a pretty oasis. The
benches facing the water looked inviting, but Jenny
didn't stop. She came to the busy shopping mall, a big
pool of light. Late shoppers were hurrying into the
Finast. Jenny dawdled, looking into the windows of
the smaller shops, seeing things she might buy if she
had the money. What did she want, though, that she
didn't already have?

Beyond the mall she walked into darkness again.
Steady traffic flowed across the bridge. Somebody
called, "Hey, Jen!" and she waved to let the driver
know she didn't want a ride. She stopped halfway
across the bridge and leaned her elbows on the iron
rail.

People didn't spend enough time looking, Uncle
Jim was right about that. There was still enough light
to see how the willows were yellowing as the spring
blood surged through them, the supple branches
reaching for the water. Here was a good place to do
some thinking, but the twilight scene was so beautiful
all she could think was how beautiful it was.

A wooden crate was serenely sailing on the slow

current. Jenny said aloud, "Oh, no!" Wasn't that a kitten clinging to a corner of the crate? All Jenny foresaw was a lot of trouble, rushing off to find men who would help her in a futile effort to rescue the kitten. As the crate came nearer she realized that her imagination had played her tricks, that some rags were caught on one corner. The current sucked the crate under the bridge. Thank God, Jenny said to herself. A kitten could never survive such a ducking.

She went back to her thinking. Why did adults like Old Doc and Mrs. Osborne assume it was right and proper that her father should find a new woman, and fall in love, and marry? Why wasn't her father satisfied? He'd had a wonderful marriage. Nobody who knew him could doubt that he had adored Martha Wren.

Jenny set her teeth, jarred by a sudden physical pain. If another woman came into the Wren house as a wife, then Martha would gradually disappear. After awhile it would be as though she had never existed.

It was hopeless, Jenny decided, to try to talk to adults. When a kid tried to communicate with them, that kid just got handed a hatful of platitudes. How about Hokie? she thought. Maybe she could talk to him.

A car stopped on the bridge and somebody called, "Jenny!" Hokie's glasses flashed in the bridge lights. She dodged through the traffic and jumped in. "Were you looking for me?" she asked.

"Yes. Your father called Dr. Everts and found out you left an hour ago."

"It was stupid for anybody to worry," she said flatly.

"Maybe so," Hokie said, "but you're such a stupid dame."

She was so shocked to hear a normal remark like that coming out of Hokie's mouth, she stared at him.

"I'm sorry," he mumbled.

"Did my father say I'm a dumb dame?"

"No, but you do take off sometimes. I mean, you go to that hollow in the field behind your house. You sit there and do nothing."

"So that makes me stupid."

"I guess not really," Hokie said mildly.

He let her out and she watched him drive away, realizing, That lad and I are beginning to have some normal conversations. She wasn't too sure about having a real intimate talk with him, though. For that, what she needed was a female friend.

She thought over those she knew and again came up with only one name, Sara Harrison. Somehow she would try to corral Sara into a real conversation. Maybe Sara would have a new slant on Jenny's hangup over this Eve Simmons thing.

11

How could you get really mad at a parent who was such a bumbler as Dr. Thomas Wren, D.V.M.? Much less, stay mad?

He did such awful things. For instance, when Jenny came home from school one afternoon she heard vague sighs and groans and woofs issuing from the woodshed. Her father as usual was helping Eben Caulfield, trying to hurry the job along. The work day ended and Dr. Tom stamped sawdust off his feet and started to wash up for supper, and Jenny said, "What's in the woodshed?"

"Oh," he said. "I almost forgot. It's old man Minatto's basset. You know, Hump."

"What's the matter with Hump?"

"He needed worming. Tape worms."

"So he's out there messing up our woodshed," Jenny said.

"I'll walk him after supper."

"Why didn't Old Man Minatto take him to the Golden Boys? They've got such lovely facilities, all that stainless steel and formica. They'd adore having that awful basset messing up their facilities."

Dr. Wren looked uncomfortable. "He's on social security."

"Hump?"

"No. Old Man Minatto. He has only two rooms in one of those River Street tenements. He called and he was crying because Hump was poorly."

"And he wanted free vet care," Jenny finished.

So who walked the dog? Jenny, naturally. Right after supper Dr. Tom got a call about a Lodge meeting that night. "Jenny, would you?" he asked, and she said, "Who else?"

She went out to the woodshed and snapped a lead on Hump's collar. He was a doll, really; his old, fat, basset body wriggled with joy like a bowlful of Jello because he loved Jenny. She started for the fields and the Osborne boys came streaming out of their house calling, "Jen, where'd you get the stuffed sausage?"

The cats joined the parade and Worthless brought up the rear, sulking, growling under his breath. They walked and walked, circling the field, until Hump got rid of his tapeworms and everything else.

At nine Doc came home from his Lodge meeting. He saw how lively Hump acted, and before Jenny got a chance to say, "That's the last time I do your dirty work for you," he said, "Jenny, you've got a noble and beautiful character." They boosted the basset into the front seat and Dr. Wren took him home.

Jenny was still in the kitchen when he returned. "Sit down, daughter," he suggested. "We'll talk."

He laid her bankbook in front of her. "I took your money out," he said. "I hated to do it, but it does save us the high interest charges. I left a small balance so your account wouldn't be wiped out. Of course I'll

97

see to it that every cent is put back, after I get to earning again."

"That's all right, Daddy," she said.

"You know I'll start putting it back the day I start practice again."

"That's all right," Jenny repeated. And it WAS all right. Just the same she felt a sinking in her stomach. It had taken many years to amass the sum that made college and vet school possible. In one more year she would finish high school, and then the money crunch would be upon them. Because how could they save? Her father practiced vet medicine on the basis of good will. The bills he didn't collect, the animals he treated for free, they weren't going to pay Jenny's board and tuition. Maybe Hump is a doll of a dog, Jenny thought, but he ain't gonna get me through college.

She stewed and fretted inside over this, but she kept her worries to herself. She had decided she didn't want any heart-to-heart talk with anyone about her other worry, either. Namely, Miss Eve Simmons.

Her relations with her best friend were becoming a wee bit strained on that score. Thursa liked to come to the Wren house after school. She helped clean the house, and she cluck-clucked over Jenny's sloppiness. And she dropped cheery remarks about people seeing Dr. Wren and Eve together. If Thursa said it once she said a dozen times how nice it was that Jenny's father had found such a nice friend.

That word "nice" set Jenny's teeth on edge. She began to wish that the town would discover that Miss

Eve Simmons was strung out on drugs or was a shop-lifter or something.

Thursa's enthusiasm grated on her to the point where she didn't want to look at Thursa's broad, friendly face. One warm day in April, when Jenny made her famous flying leap onto the bus and took the seat Thursa had saved, Thursa said, "It's a such a nice day, I'll come to your house and we'll start your spring cleaning. We'll start on the attic."

"Maybe I can't," Jenny said. "Maybe I'm going to dig Indian relics."

"Who with?"

"Sara Harrison." Jenny wasn't making this up en-tirely out of whole cloth. Last fall, Sara had men-tioned to Jenny that her family had unearthed some unusual objects on their property. Come spring, Sara said, they planned a real dig. Anything like that fascinated Jenny, and she had said, "Hey, that sounds like fun!"

"If you want to dig too, that would be great," Sara had said.

Luckily, Jenny remembered this conversation now. She certainly had no desire to tackle the Wrens' attic.

When Jenny approached Sara in math class and said, "Hey, last fall you mentioned you might dig for Indian relics," Sara was delighted. They made a date for that afternoon. Jenny would stay for supper and somebody would bring her home afterward.

Jenny called her house. "Pops, I won't be there to fix your supper. You can scrounge in the refrigerator," she told her father.

Sara's bus let them out at the Harrisons' lane. They lived in a big farmhouse, and Jenny felt right at home because it was shabby and untidy like her own house. Dr. Harrison, a chemistry professor, spent his weekdays in New York. His wife stayed home and wrote books; she was a clinical psychologist. Two of Sara's brothers were away at college, but Jonas was temporarily living at home, a hairy dropout from college.

The family raised its own organic food, Sara explained, leading Jenny through a tangle of tall, dead weeds to last summer's vegetable garden. The girls carried shovels and Jonas trailed after, mournfully blowing on a trumpet.

He became interested too, and joined in the dig. These Harrisons obviously knew what they were doing. They suspected that the potato patch was the site of an old Indian camp. It was lucky Jenny wasn't afraid of snakes because there were plenty of them among the weeds. What she got was a short, intense course in artifacts. Sara and Jonas pounced on what looked like plain stones and shards, which turned out to be axes or pestles or arrowheads when washed in a bucket of water. Jenny found a nice axe head and a couple of flint arrowheads. She added them to the Harrisons' collection but they said No, finder's keepers; she should take them home.

"Ma will have a fit when she sees her potato patch," Jonas mentioned. "It looks like No Man's Land."

"We've got to go deeper," his sister told him. "This site may be on top of an older campsite. Ma will have to find another place for her potatoes."

It was six o'clock when they quit. Sara poured Jenny an orange drink — carrot juice — which tasted awful. Jonas pounded on his mother's study door. "Ma, we're hungry!" he yelled.

"Go away!" she yelled back. "Dig some dandelions!"

They took a pail and some knives and crawled around on what passed for the Harrisons' front lawn, digging dandelion greens. Again Jonas pounded on his mother's door. "Ma, we've got the greens; we're starving!" She emerged, smiling cheerfully.

She wore an Indian-print smock, and her hair was drawn severely back and knotted in a frowzy bun. There was nothing casual about the way she went about cooking the dinner. It seemed as though she had a dozen hands and the pots and pans flew through the air. In a few minutes a delicious meal was on the table, steamed dandelion greens, mushrooms, thick slabs of garlic bread, cheese, and red wine. Afterward Jonas offered to take Jenny home on his Honda. She was thinking how great this would be, how it would shake her father up when she came roaring in, but Mrs. Harrison vetoed the idea. "Absolutely not," she stated. "This child's blood is not going to be spilled all over the highway. You'll take her in the car." Jonas did as he was told.

That visit gave Jenny a lot to think about. Some people in Harley put the Harrisons down as odd and alien, but to Jenny they seemed utterly wonderful. She began seeing a lot of Sara.

She asked her once if she and Jonas really intended

101

to be archaeologists. "Jonas might," Sara said. "Wearing sandals and slopping around Africa or somewhere is probably his bag. I doubt it's mine. I'm keeping my options open." Jenny thought, I ought to keep my options open too. Then she realized, I don't have any options; I only want to be a vet.

The new hospital was taking shape fast. The framing was finished, the siding and roof were on. A spell of wet weather came in May, but the building was enclosed, so Eben Caulfield could work inside. The hammering went on steadily while Eben sang to himself in a nasal monotone.

People took a lively interest, especially owners of Dr. Tom's patients. A woman called one day. "I'm Abby Sykes," she announced. "Your daddy treated my cat Mossie for blood in the urine."

"Oh, sure," Jenny said. She was expected to remember every animal and its ailments.

"Cystitis isn't easy to clear up. Those two young squirts at their so-called clinic couldn't do it. But your daddy did. It's painful. Nobody but me knows how Mossie suffered."

"I guess that's right," Jenny agreed.

"That's not the reason why I called."

Jenny hoped she would get to the reason soon. Hokie was waiting for her to come and help plant the vegetable garden out back beyond the hospital.

"I've got two wicker chairs and a settee and a wicker table," Mrs. Sykes said. "I was toting them over to my neighbor's tag sale, today, when it occurred to me your daddy could use them, so I toted them home again. They're his, for his waiting room. The only thing is, the cushions are faded. Now, Jenny, I've got some nice chintz. My daughter bought it for drapes, then decided the pattern was too loud. I'm going to re-cover the cushions for the chairs and the settee and make your daddy some nice pleated drapes for his waiting room."

This was indeed a handsome offer. "That's just too MUCH, Mrs. Sykes!" Jenny exclaimed.

"What if he doesn't like the pattern, after I get 'em made?"

"Daddy will think it's great," Jenny assured her. "He doesn't know from nothing about interior decorating!"

Mrs. Sykes said that was all right; a man who could cure painful ailments like her Mossie's cystitis shouldn't be expected to be an interior decorator too.

Jenny was glad she had some cheerful news for her father. He was steadying sheets of plasterboard while Eben nailed them. "It's nice of Mrs. Sykes and Mossie," he said.

"Let's hope the furniture isn't too awful."

"We can only hope," he said with a grin. He didn't do much smiling these days because he too was appalled by the way the money was going out and none was coming in.

She went then and helped Hokie. He marked shallow trenches with a hoe, and she scattered the radish, bush beans, and lettuce seeds, and he covered them up.

He asked about the artifacts digging, and Jenny told

him Mrs. Harrison had forbidden any further exavating during the summer. They had to wait until her potatoes had been harvested.

Hokie had a disconcerting way of switching subjects. "How do you feel about Bartók?" he asked.

"What's a Bartók?" Jenny Demanded.

"I see I still haven't plumbed the depths of your ignorance," Hokie said mildly. "He's a composer. I thought you might come to my house tomorrow to hear my new records, if you have nothing better to do."

She could have thought of a dozen better things to do but she said, "Sure. Great." This was really a first: Hokie Jones inviting somebody to his house.

Dr. Wren had overheard this conversation, and when the long day was over and they were alone he mentioned it. "Jen, you'll make a human being out of that lad yet. I just hope you live through his Bartóks. Those LPs can be very long indeed."

"Nobody's ever set foot inside Hokie's house," Jenny told him. "I can't wait to see it. His parents aren't very sociable. Maybe that's why Hokie comes here so often."

"Don't you know why Hokie spends practically all his waking hours here?" Dr. Wren asked.

"What do you mean?"

"He's in love with you."

Disbelief sharpened Jenny's tone. "Dad, that's just plain stupid!"

"That boy is so much in love with you he's deaf, dumb, and blind," Dr. Wren said.

12

That statement of her father's caught Jenny by surprise. Oh, she had wondered lately if she really saw what she thought she saw in Hokie's eyes. She said the first thing that came into her head. "It's just Pinhead Jones, and who cares?" she stammered.

"I care quite a lot," her father said coldly. "I'm very fond of that boy. In this world you don't often encounter a person who is purely kind and good, and that seems to be Hokie's case. Love's not such a common commodity, any of us can afford to throw it away." He stalked into the house.

That night sleep would not come. Jenny was mulling over the change in her relationship with Hokie. It was the change in her relationship with her father that really bugged her, though.

She was remembering the olden days when she and her father had lived together so simply, sharing the work and jokes and planning a really great future. Now that future looked awfully iffy. If Eve Simmons married the doctor and moved in, what happened to Jenny's place in the home? If the money couldn't be saved, what happened to Jenny's prospects for an expensive education?

Her father too seemed confused, mixed up. For instance, he had stopped carrying the dilapidated bag that Jenny's mother had given him long ago as a Christmas gift. Miss Simmons had presented him with a new one, and he had packed it with his instruments and drugs. Jenny had thought the old one was gone forever. Recently, however, she had found it in his closet, carefully oiled and wrapped in plastic. He couldn't bring himself to throw it away.

Not long ago she had asked him, "Did you notice Mother's tulips? They're nicer than ever this year." He had only grunted, but when he went outside he moved along the flower border which Martha Wren had lovingly tended. He stooped and brushed out some dead leaves Jenny had missed, and on his face was the familiar look of suffering.

So how come, when he dressed for a date with Eve, his face put on a look of such bright expectancy? It was the same face!

His remark about Hokie being in love with her had one result; Jenny stopped baiting Hokie. She adopted a policy of wait and see. When he came to fetch her on Sunday, she was unusually quiet and mild.

The Jones lived on Dr. Everts's street where the grand houses were. Theirs too was set back in its own small park of lawn and trees. The house was older than Old Doc's, a white clapboard with a beautiful doorway, which was one of Harley's famous sights.

There had always been plenty of money in the Jones family. Mrs. Jones employed help, but they said around town that she never did anything but stay home and clean. When Jenny stepped across the threshold she saw the results. The serene rooms were filled with beautiful antiques, and everything was spotless. Jenny thought, Thursa ought to see this; she'd find out what clean really means!

It was equally clear the other story was true: that a guest was a rare event. Hokie's parents waited in big chairs on either side of the drawing room fireplace. As soon as the introductions were over, the maid brought in the tea.

Now this maid was none other than Thursa's cousin Anna. Jenny had heard she worked for Mrs. Jones, but she never thought of her as anybody's maid; she was just Anna. In her shiny black dress, stiff white apron and cap, though, she was a stranger. "Hey, Anna!" Jenny exclaimed. Anna only gave her a tiny smile and helped Mrs. Jones serve the tea.

Jenny tried again when Anna brought her cup. "Hey, Anna, have you seen Thursa lately?"

"No, I haven't, Jenny," Anna said quietly.

Mr. and Mrs. Jones were tall, thin, gray people, courteous, careful people. The tea party was a silent one. Hokie sat beside Jenny on the sofa, balancing his plate and cup. His mouth twitched with amusement, as though he was enjoying the encounter. Jenny had two of the thin, flat almond cookies. Then Mrs. Jones said, "You young people wish to enjoy Homer's new records," and Anna took their cups, and the tea party was over.

"Who's Homer?" Jenny muttered out of the side of her mouth.

"It is I; I am Homer," Hokie muttered out of the side of his.

To Jenny's surprise, he led her upstairs to his room. "How come your parents let us go to your room?" she asked.

"They decided that the proprieties would be observed if the door was left open," he told her.

"Do you have to talk like a stupid dictionary?" Jenny demanded.

The door was duly left open, but Jenny couldn't keep her remarks to herself. "Hoke, they're something else!" she burst out. "In fact, you're something else!"

"I know," Hokie said mildly. "We're probably the last of the red-hot Puritans."

Jenn's laugh rang out. She was truly appreciating Hokie Jones today; he WAS something else, but whatever it was she liked it.

The Bartók, however, was awful. It went on and on and didn't make any sense. Jenny had no desire to appear uncouth and ignorant, but enough was enough, and when Hokie got up to put on the second record she had to protest. "Hokie, I'm afraid I've got a tin ear. I mean, your Bartók is just great and I hope you and he will be very happy together. But haven't you got any rock?"

"No," he said. "Do you know that sea expression, 'shiver my timbers?' I've often thought that a good loud rock record would really shiver some timbers around here."

"Hokie, how do you stand it?"

"Do you mean the house?"

"Yes, of course I mean the house."

"Except that you mean my parents, too. I love my parents," Hokie said simply.

"Of course you do!"

"There's no 'of course' about it," Hokie said. "Lots of kids hate their parents. I don't. Now we'll go to see the coach house, the rabbits, and my trains. I warned my mother I was going to show you the sights, and she went into a real frenzy of cleaning."

Jenny saw the sights, and she was awed. The immaculate coach house held a western-type coach, a beautiful thing, a museum thing, shiny and varnished. It also contained a sleigh, a surrey, Mr. Jones's gleaming black Cadillac and Hokie's Volkswagen. The latter looked humble indeed in its elegant surroundings.

They went on to the rabbits. No simple hutches for them; the sleek, fat creatures had small white cottages and big runs. And Hokie's trains occupied their own building. Jenny was entranced by the miniature village of houses, trees, stores, stations, switching yards, signals. Actually she was speechless. There was too much to take in all at once.

She noticed two work coats and two engineers' caps hung on hooks. "My father and I play trains together," Hokie explained.

They returned to the house. The parents were reading in the same chairs by the fireplace. "I had a lovely time, and I thank you very much," Jenny told her hostess.

Mrs. Jones's thin lips parted just a bit in a sweet smile and she said, "Perhaps you will come again."

Jenny burst out, as soon as the car was moving, "Hokie, I like your folks! And your place is wonderful. I don't see why you don't have people in. They'd jump at the chance, if they were invited. You ought to socialize."

"We don't know how," Hokie said.

"I wonder why they named you Homer."

"It's the cross I have to bear," he said. "You could really do me in, Jenny, if you called me that at school."

"I would never do a thing like that," she assured him.

She studied him during the ride home. Why did the kids call him "Pinhead"? His was nicely shaped. Maybe any head would look small on top of such a tall body, because you had to look up so far in order to see it.

The next day she was still wondering about this. Why did the kids try to put Hokie down? When noon came, Thursa wouldn't go to the cafeteria because she was dieting. Jenny bought a sandwich and some milk and joined her under a tree on the lawn. Thursa ate an apple but eyed Jenny's tunafish sandwich longingly. "People are wrong about Hokie Jones," Jenny announced. "I mean, why do the kids put him down? Just because he's smarter?"

"I always thought he was nice," Thursa said. "What kind of a time did you have yesterday?"

"Great!"

Sara was crossing the grass, and Thursa said gloomily, "I suppose I'd better leave you and your wonderful intellectual friend, so you can have a wonderful intellectual conversation."

Jenny held Thursa's chubby arm firmly and repeated her remark about Hokie. Thursa shrugged and said it was the other kids' loss if they didn't appreciate Hokie.

Jenny had let herself get roped into a meeting of the Drama Club that afternoon. It took place in the art room after school, and no sooner had it started than Jenny found she was bored. They were talking about putting on a play called "Little Mary Sunshine." Jenny was sitting with Enid Kaplan, and Enid said, "There's that Hokie Jones. What's he doing here?"

Jenny glanced back. Hokie was leaning his tall frame against the wall. She wanted to call, "Hey, Hoke, sit with us," but she didn't. That would be declaring to the entire school populace that she and he were going together. Instead she said, "Hokie's a professional, so I don't know why he would want to mess around with a bunch of amateurs."

Carl Hanson in the row ahead heard that. "What do you mean, Jen?"

"He works with the Creative Arts League."

113

"That bunch of creeps!"

"Maybe they are, maybe they aren't, but Hokie isn't any creep."

Her remark just sort of hung there. She had given herself away, and she could guess what would happen. "It's Jenny Wren and Hokie Jones now, how do you like that?" people would say.

The meeting only got duller as it went along. Jenny stood up, hoping to slip out unobtrusively, but Enid asked, "Where are you going?"

"Home," Jenny said. "I don't think amateur theatricals are my bag." In her haste she fell over a boy's sprawled legs, and he caught her from falling.

Hokie was still leaning against the wall and followed her out. They climbed into his Volks and started home. "What were you doing at that dumb meeting?" Jenny asked.

"I was there because you were there," he told her. "I've got to talk to you. Jen, I heard that you really fouled up on that last physics test. What's the matter with you?"

"I don't know," she said. "I just don't connect with things like I used to."

"Problems at home?"

"Problems," she agreed.

"Jen, you've got to start to connect or you'll have a bigger problem. You won't get into a college that offers good pre-med unless you keep your grades up."

"I guess, I guess," she said impatiently. She didn't need a lecture from Hokie; she knew she had fouled up on the physics.

13

She was getting along a lot better with Mr. Caulfield than she had ever expected to. Their relationship had started badly, with both wearing large chips on their shoulders, but it had improved. She went out one day to give him a message from the lumber yard. He was nailing sheets of plasterboard, sheathing the hospital waiting room. She stayed to watch because it was fascinating — the speedy way he popped nails out of his mouth and hammered them in.

A car appeared in the drive and a couple of hippie-type men got out, one carrying something wrapped in a towel. He unfolded it, and she recognized the big bird as a flicker. "It's wing's broken," he explained.

"The doctor's not here," Jenny began.

Eben never missed anything that went on at the Wrens' place. "The doctor ain't here but I am, and I can set a wing good as the doc can," he announced. "Fetch me some tape and some tongue depressors, Jenny."

She did so, but the phone was ringing and she had to go back to the house. Twice more she started out to see how the wing-setting was getting along, but each time the phone called her back. The men and the bird were gone when she was finally free. "How did it go?" she asked Eben.

"Easy as rolling off a log," he told her. Then he stuffed his mouth full of nails, and that was the end of any conversation.

This was a Saturday. Jenny didn't care much for Saturday nights. She had been hoping Hokie would ask her out. Her father and his ladylove usually went somewhere on that night which was sacred to dating. He was eating in, however, so she made a tunafish salad. She told him about the bird. "Mr. Caulfield's cutting in on your territory," she commented.

"Everybody wants to get into the act," he said, smiling at her.

She didn't smile back. "What's the matter, Jen?" he asked.

"Oh, I don't know."

"You must know. You haven't acted like yourself for days. Weeks, really. What's on your mind, honey?"

She couldn't say, "My money had to go into the hospital, so now I don't see how I'll ever get through college." No, she couldn't open up that can of worms because he'd think she had no confidence in him. She reluctantly opened up the other can of worms. "I suppose it's Eve," she said. "I mean, you know, Dad, any girl would feel funny about another woman taking her mother's place."

There, it was out.

He was too intelligent a father to shout heartily, "Nonsense!" and he was too decent a father to get

116

mad. Instead he said slowly, "I know. Well, maybe I
don't know, but I can imagine. You and your mother
were very close, and you can't bear the idea of anyone
taking her place."

Jenny nodded. Worthless, sensitive to his family's
moods, came and put his black nose in Jenny's hand.
She bent and kissed the top of his head. He went
around the table and tried the same thing and Dr.
Wren absently rubbed his ears. "I'm glad that it's out,
how you feel," Dr. Wren said. "The situation is,
though, that nobody could ever take your mother's
place. Nobody. Eve knows that."

"She'd move in," Jenny said, her voice trembling.
"She'd cook in the same pots and pans. She'd take
care of my mother's flowers. She'd sleep in my
mother's bed."

"Jenny, it's my bed too," he said quietly. "You
don't doubt how much I loved your mother?"

Jenny shook her head, unable to speak. "I still have
a lot of years ahead of me," her father went on. "I
have to have some sort of a life. But nothing between
you and me will change."

He came to her and held her head against him
and smoothed her hair. "I have to go," he said. "I'm
keeping Eve waiting. I'm glad we talked. I hope
and pray you and Eve will come around to being
friends."

When he drove off, she was sitting on the stone step
outside the kitchen door. She was still sitting there
when Thursa, dateless too, appeared. Jenny was so
silent, Thursa didn't stay long. She didn't get mad;

she said, "I guess you've got an awful headache or something," and stood up to leave.

Usually Jenny would have said, "I'll go with you," because usually they walked each other halfway home. Jenny made no move; she just said, "Okay," and sat there, hugging her knees.

She went to bed feeling sad and woke in the morning feeling sad. She hoped that Thursa would come and help pass the time or that Sara would call with an invitation to the Harrisons' farm. She and her father puttered around, doing odd jobs, but they didn't talk much. After lunch he left.

Jenny roused herself and walked through the house. It was messy, needing a thorough turning out. She fetched the vacuum cleaner from the closet, plugged it in, and turned on the motor. Then she turned off the motor, unplugged it, and put it back in the closet. The dirt wouldn't run away; it would hang around until she felt more like coping with it.

She was brooding, lackadaisically combing Hannibal's thick fur, when Hokie showed up. "I thought I'd work on that desk in the woodshed, the one Mr. Hall gave your dad," Hokie explained. "After it's sandpapered and varnished, it'll do fine for the office."

"Sometimes I get the feeling people think we're on relief, the way they dump old furniture on us," Jenny complained.

"It's not that way, and you know it," Hokie said. "They just want to help get the business started again."

Jenny was startled when soon after a police car

118

whirled into the driveway. Hokie ran out of the wood-shed. "Jenny, where's your father?" Officer Shedd called. "I'm supposed to meet him here."

"What's up?" she asked.

He didn't have time to answer, for Dr. Wren's car appeared, Eve on the seat beside him. "Jen, get my bag," the doctor ordered.

She brought it. "What's going on?" Hokie asked.

"It's some sort of a mess at the mobile-home park," the doctor told him. "Apparently some animals have been abandoned. You kids can come if you want to."

Officer Shedd in his car led the way out Route 102 to the mobile-home park, which some Harley people called "The Eyesore." He took several turns down narrow lanes between the close-packed trailers. A small crowd was waiting.

One man acted as spokesman. "We hear her cats in there," he said. "We haven't seen this Mrs. Clemm for several days. At least that's what she calls herself. We never saw a Mr. Clemm —"

"Does the manager of the park have a key?" Officer Shedd interrupted.

"I don't know. We hardly ever see him."

The officer tried the door. They heard a faint bark and crying, and Eve begged, "Please, please, open the door and see what's wrong."

The stout metal door didn't yield. One of the neigh-bors brought a crowbar. Officer Shedd said, "I've got no warrant so I'm asking for trouble; I'll probably be charged with breaking and entering." He inserted the crowbar in the crack. Other men joined him, leaning

119

on it. The door gave suddenly, its hinges sprung. Then everybody moved back, for a terrible odor poured out.

A small shaggy dog tumbled out and lay whimpering on the packed earth. Eve gathered it in her arms. They peered through the door at an appalling mess, but nobody stepped forward because the smell was so thick it was like an evil curtain.

Eve handed the puppy to a woman and asked her to give it food and water. The woman took it because Eve seemed to speak with the voice of authority, but she exclaimed, "Ugh! It stinks!" Jenny took it, afraid she was going to drop it. It had no weight; it was literally skin and bones.

They were waiting for someone to make a move. "We can't stand here forever," Dr. Wren said.

"After you, sir," Officer Shedd agreed. They gagged and choked, going around sliding open the windows. The others crowded into the living room. Jenny was still clutching the puppy because she didn't know what to do with it.

Clothes, furniture, curtains, broken dishes, mattresses, newspapers were tossed around crazily. Everything was permeated by the stench of excrement and stale urine. A canary lay on its back, dead in its cage. Dead fish floated in a tank green with slime. Beyond they glimpsed the kitchen, a shambles of open tin cans, broken glass, and dishes and pans foul and furry with spoiled food.

There was a squawk of terror and a Siamese cat shot past Jenny. Hokie caught it and clutched it. It was lath-thin. It hissed and yowled, its blue eyes blazing red with fright.

Eve stood in the midst of the awful confusion, shouting, "There's a cat! And another! Somebody, shut the door so they won't run away!"

"I'm getting out of here," a man said. "My stomach won't take this." Several of the neighbors followed him. "Let the police handle it," another said, and someone added, "They ought to burn the place just the way it is." They filed out but they didn't go away.

Dr. Wren slid shut the screen door again. Then he called to those outside, "Do any of you have cat carriers?"

"I do," one woman offered.

"Listen, Ethel, you can't put those cats in the same box you carry your Toughie in," a friend protested.

"Go get the box," Officer Shedd ordered.

Ethel, a wide woman in red pants, obediently started off. "Don't do it, Mrs. Sullivan," a man advised. "That cop's got no right to order us around."

She hesitated. Everyone was watching her. She squared her heavy shoulders and said, "You can have my carrier. And you can bring that dog and that cat to my home. I'll feed 'em. And furthermore, I'm ashamed of the lot of you!" She glared at her friends and marched away.

Eve seemed to have taken charge. "Go with her, will you, Jenny, you and Hokie?" she asked. "Take the puppy and the cat."

They did as they were told. Jenny was numbed

because looking into that place was like catching a vision of hell. "What kind of people live in filth like that?" she said to Hokie as they followed Mrs. Sullivan. "Like animals? No, that's wrong. Animals hate filth."

Mrs. Sullivan was still sputtering about her neighbors as she unlocked her door for Jenny and Hokie. The cat darted away and hid. She began opening cans and filling bowls with food.

The pup emptied the water bowl first, then started on the food. Jenny snatched up the dish. "Let's give it to him slowly, so he won't throw it up," she suggested.

The dog gobbled what she gave him, a spoonful at a time, then sat down and cried for more. Seeing him eating, the Siamese emerged and hunched over a dish, snarling, lashing out with sable paws at anyone who came close.

"You kids don't have to stay," Mrs. Sullivan said. "I'll look after these. But you can't leave them here. One cat or dog, that's all we're allowed at this park and I've already got my Toughie."

The neighbors still stood around, watching the Clemm trailer from a distance. Jenny dreaded the thought of re-entering that hell hole, but she had no choice. Eve Simmons was in there, so Jenny couldn't hang back. Dr. Wren and the cop were heaving stuff and swearing. Another shrieking Siamese darted past Jenny and vanished into a pile in a corner. They heard cries and scrabbling noises.

Eve was sobbing, tugging at some stinking pillows,

turning them over. Dr. Wren tried to pull her away. "Stop it, Eve!"

"They're under here. I know!"

"Listen, Eve, this isn't working. They're so frightened they just dash from one place to another — "

"Come here, Doc!" Officer Shedd called. They stumbled through the trailer to find him. The small bedroom was chaotic like the rest of the place, the mattress pulled off the bed, dirty clothes flung around. An orange tiger cat cowered beside some dead kittens. It wasn't the animals the officer had called them to see, it was words scrawled in scarlet lipstick on the wall, "Don't follow, you'll be sorry, don't follow, don't follow." The red trail of words ran around the room.

"She's either awful sick or awful crazy or both," the cop said, his voice shaking. "The manager will have her car number. I'll ask the State Police to put out an APB. That woman needs help."

He went off to question the manager and to talk to the State Police over his car radio. The others were left with the dreadful task of picking over the piles, trying to corral the starving cats. Dr. Wren was giving Jenny and Eve troubled looks. "This is no place for you girls," he said. "You'll get sick. Let Hokie and me try to round them up."

Eve ignored that. "It might be easier to lure them out," she suggested. "Jenny, would you ask those horrible people if they have any pet food that's fishy? Tuna or mackerel? The smell might bring the cats out of the piles. And ask for boxes and some bits of string.

They might at least be willing to part with some boxes and string!"

Dr. Wren said again, "Eve, you've got to let Hokie and me cope. Officer Shedd will help."

She looked him in the eye and said, "No."

A man was banging on the door. "I'm Staats; I'm the manager of this park!" he called. He stuck his head in, then fell back and said, "Jeez."

"I wouldn't brag about that!" Dr. Wren barked. "The Health Officer will have to close down the whole place if this is the way you manage!"

"I'll have the lot of you up on trespass charges!" Mr. Staats roared back.

"Tell that to the cop out there in his car," Dr. Wren ordered.

Staats wavered. "This is pretty awful," he admitted. "That Ramona Clemm has given trouble in the past, drunk and disorderly, stuff like that. Maybe the only way to clean this place is to douse it with kerosene and set it afire."

"Not until we get the animals out," Eve told him. "Jenny will you try to get the cans of fish and some boxes?"

Jenny and Hokie left, but not before they heard Staats tell Eve, "This is no place for a lady like you."

"This is exactly the place for a lady like me!" Eve snapped back.

They knocked on doors and collected boxes and some rope. One elderly woman invited them in. "I haven't any cat food; but I've got tuna for humans at sixty cents a can and you're welcome to it," she told

124

them. "What are you going to do with the cats, after you catch them? I saw Ethel Sullivan took two into her place. You can bring one here for a little while, but you can't leave it. I don't like cats." She opened the cans of tuna and provided paper plates. They thanked her and left.

"What are we going to do with the animals?" Hokie asked Jenny. "That's beginning to bug me."

"The Humane Society will come from Moss City and take them," Jenny told him.

"Then what happens to them?"

"They'll try to place them. The pup and the Siamese will get homes, but I don't know about the other cats. If they're sick, the Humane Society will put them down."

"How?"

"Gas chamber,"

"They deserve better, after what they've been through," Hokie protested.

Jenny could tell by the sick look on his face that this whole thing was really getting to him. "We'll probably take some, and maybe Old Doc will take some in," she told him.

As they neared the Clemm trailer, two State Police cars passed them. The officers joined Jerry Shedd. Outside, where the air smelled sweet. Hokie knocked on the door, and called, "Dr. Wren, open up and let us in."

The cops approached. The park people were drifting back, and Jenny thought, disgusted, A little Sunday excitement, that's all this means to them.

Hoke and Jenny slipped inside. A cop with a sergeant's badge announced, "We're coming in too."

"No!" Eve shouted, and planted herself in the doorway.

"What do you mean, 'No,' lady?" the sergeant demanded.

Eve lowered her voice. "You'll have to wait. I don't question your authority, and of course you have to investigate. The woman's obviously ill and has to be found. But right now we have all we can handle. If you come in you'll make our job impossible."

She turned to those inside. "Tom, four of us in here are too many. If you and Hokie left, I think Jenny and I would have a better chance. Jenny, would you be willing to stay?"

What else could Jenny say? "Sure. Okay."

Dr. Wren started to argue but Eve told him, "We'll try it my way," and gently pushed him out and slid the bolt on the door.

Her hair had tumbled out of its pins, her face was smudged, and she looked like a crazy woman, herself. Jenny was utterly confused by the change from the calm, beautiful Eve Simmons she had known. This Eve had a lot of nerve; she didn't hesitate, she acted. She did the right thing in an emergency. Jenny wasn't at all sure that she herself might not have backed away from this horrible mess. "You stood them off pretty good, Eve," she said.

They set plates of cat food around, swept chairs clear of rubbish, and sat down to wait. Eve shuddered. "We'll never get this smell off," she said. "A thousand baths will never get us clean."

She caught her breath. "Jenny, a cat is coming up behind you. Let it start to eat, and then grab it. Once you get your hands on it, don't let go."

Jenny sat perfectly still as a gray cat glided past her feet. Its attention was totally riveted on the food. Jenny made her grab. The cat raked her arm, but she hung on.

Eve was holding the box. Jenny pushed the cat in and they frantically folded down the top and flung rope around it. The cat howled, clawing at the cardboard. Eve unbolted the door, thrust the box out, and ordered, "Hokie, put it in the car and shut the windows. This one will fight its way free in no time." She bolted the door again.

Seeing this bit of action, the police converged on the door and began banging. "This is ridiculous, Miss Simmons!" the sergeant called.

Dr. Wren added his voice. "Eve, please let me in to help."

"No," she said. "Our plan is working."

"Look at Jenny's arms," Dr. Wren suggested.

Eve did, and said, "Oh, dear God, this place is filthy and she'll get a terrible infection." Then Eve sobbed and tears poured down her dirty face.

"To hell with that," Jenny said. "Our plan's working. Another cat is eating out of that dish in the kitchen."

They caught a half-grown tiger and secured it in a box. This one only cried plaintively. Jenny carried it to the door.

The elderly woman who had given Jenny and Hokie the cans of tuna took the box. "I've changed my mind," she said. "Maybe I could use a cat. What is it?"

"It's a little tiger," Jenny told her.

"A tiger cat will do me fine." She went off with her prize.

The spring dusk was coming down and Eve snapped on the lights. Another hour went by. The men had given up yelling orders and waited quietly. Jenny and Eve caught six more, two Siamese, a yellow tiger, two half-grown black and whites, and a calico. One cat raked Eve across the face while they were getting it into a box, and Eve let out a few well-chosen swear words. Their arms were a bloody mess and Jenny's throbbed with pain.

They listened and heard nothing. "I think we've got them all," Eve said. They searched, using curtain rods to poke into corners and turn over the filthy piles. They found one more dead cat. They saw no movement, and Eve said, "I'm satisfied. Are you?"

"I'm satisfied," Jenny said.

They emerged. The men stared at them, horrified. "You'd better take them straight to the hospital, Doc," the sergeant said. "They need tetanus shots right away."

Dr. Wren nodded. "Come, Eve, Jenny."

"Where's Hokie?" Jenny asked.

"One of the officers drove him and all the cats to our house."

"How about the pup, and the cat we left with Mrs. Sullivan?"

"Hokie will come back for them."

"I'm going to take the pup home to my kid," Officer Shedd put in.

Dr. Wren put one arm around Eve and the other around Jenny and led them to the car.

14

They caused a sensation at the hospital, and when a nurse took them to a john, Jenny saw why. They both looked like witches, their hair tangled and matted, their clothes filthy, their arms bloody. Eve had a really bad scratch across her face. They dabbed at the dirt as best they could with paper towels. Dr. Janelli was waiting for them in the emergency room. He looked at them and then at Dr. Wren and said, "Where were you when the battle was going on, Doc?"

"I always let my women do my fighting for me," Dr. Wren said grimly.

The nurse cleaned their wounds and the doctor treated the scratches and gave them tetanus shots and antibiotic shots to ward off infection. Then Jenny's father took them home.

Riding home in the back seat through the dark town, Jenny thought how quiet and lovely the ordinary world seemed and what a difference a few hours could make. For weeks she and Eve had been "That woman and I." Now suddenly they were "We."

There was a lot to do when they arrived, although Jenny only longed to go to bed. Hokie was coping as best he could. The Wren animals were shut in the woodshed. The starved cats were hunched over plates on the kitchen floor. Hokie held the pup, feeding it pieces of hot dog.

Dr. Wren surveyed the place, carpeted with cats. "I count nine," he said. "What do you get?"

"I get nine, too," Hokie said.

"Jenny, call your Uncle Jim and tell him it's his Christian duty to take some of these off our hands," Dr. Wren ordered.

Jenny rang the number and explained the emergency. Dr. Everts didn't give her any argument. "They're not to be put down," she warned. "They've had an awful time."

He asked if they were nice cats, and she said they would be, after they'd put some flesh on their bones and the stink had blown off them. "It's hard to find homes for grown cats," he said.

"That isn't exactly news to me," she told him, and hung up.

She was wondering how she was going to feed her human guests. Hoke had grandly handed out her supply of hot dogs to the animals. Her father solved that problem. Officer Shedd called to say that he was coming to get his puppy, and Dr. Wren asked him to pick up a large pizza at the Pizza Palace.

Jenny made coffee and fixed a tossed salad. While they waited for the cop and their supper, they moodily surveyed the cats, who had perched on the counters and were washing their faces. "Hoke can take one Siamese and the two black and whites to Uncle Jim," Jenny suggested.

"I'll take the yellow tiger," Eve offered.

132

"Pets aren't allowed at your place," Dr. Wren reminded her.

"What the landlord doesn't know won't hurt him. I can stash her in a closet when other tenants drop in."

"I'll take the calico," Hokie offered.

"How about your mother?" Jenny asked.

"It's like Miss Simmons says, what my mother doesn't know won't hurt her," Hokie said. "I'll keep it in the train barn."

At last Officer Shedd came, carrying the big flat box. Jenny set it in the middle of the table and they fell to.

Who would ever have expected to see the sophisticated Miss Simmons gnawing a wedge of pizza? Jenny was still having trouble accepting the fact that Eve was apparently just a nice human being who had quite a remarkable collection of swear words. "What about that scratch on your face, Eve?" she asked. "Will you go to school tomorrow?"

"Yes," Eve said. "I'll tell the principal, 'You should see the other guy!' "

They asked Officer Shedd about Mrs. Clemm. An APB had been sent out, he said. The cops were going through the mobile home, hoping to turn up a letter or some clue. "She's too sick to be roaming around," he said. "She probably needs both medical and psychiatric help."

He thanked them for the supper and left, carrying his dog. Dr. Wren took the exhausted Eve and her cat home. Hokie helped Jenny clean up the kitchen and wanted to linger to talk over the events of the day, but

Jenny told him she needed a bath and some shut-eye. She helped him get Dr. Everts's cats into her carrier, and he took his calico and departed.

At last the house was silent. Jenny leaned her elbows on the kitchen table, too tired to move. The four cats that the Wrens had won in the raffle stared at her, the two Siamese lashing their sinuous tails. She summoned up the energy to fix them a litter pan, and left them.

A hot bath and shampoo made her feel somewhat better; at least she got rid of the smell. She fell into bed.

A chorus broke out downstairs, Siamese wails and the plain cats' mournful cries. Jenny tried to close her ears but she had to give in. Her father would soon be home and he needed a night's sleep, too. She marched downstairs and yelled, "Shut up!" The silence was deafening. "Shut up and come with me," she ordered, and marched upstairs again.

She switched off her light and soon felt warm presences on the bed. Four bodies were pressed against her. The minute they were touched, her bedmates started to purr. Lulled by that contented thunder, she dozed off.

She didn't sleep well. Her arms hurt and so did her butt where the doctor had injected the tetanus antitoxin. Several times she awoke from vague nightmares. The reason was clear; the cats on the bed had brought with them the sickening odor from the trailer. If the incident was over she could forget it, but it wouldn't end until the woman was found.

She had heard the cops talking about similar cases, about people who willingly lived in filth. "It's some kind of psychosis," one cop said. "Usually it's a senile psychosis. But this woman is young."

Jenny re-lived the time she had sat quietly with Eve, waiting for the starving cats to emerge. She had overheard Hokie saying, "Dr. Wren, that Miss Simmons is okay. I mean, she's great."

When they got home to the Wren house Eve had taken time to wash and to comb her hair neatly. Jenny remembered her, though, as a wild woman, sobbing and swearing, determined to get her own way, to get the animals out of that awful place. She set up like cement, Jenny thought. She stood off all those cops.

Jenny was still very tired the next morning, and very reluctant to face the new day.

The balance had shifted between her and her father and Eve, and that was the truth. She couldn't put Eve down as just a clever woman who was trying to snag Dr. Tom and march him up the well-known aisle. Eve wasn't a stereotype Jenny had to deal with, the scheming female. She was real. And dammit! Jenny thought, if I don't watch my step I'll start to like her.

The morning started out like a typical Monday snafu, only this one was worse. Jenny staggered downstairs, the newcomers trailing after her. She fixed the morning meal and let in her own brood. Worthless was horrified to realize how the cat population had swelled overnight, and the Wren cats set upon the intruders. There ensued a free-for-all, and the howls and screams brought Dr. Wren on the run.

Jenny threw the Wren cats out and pushed the new cats into the downstairs bedroom. Worthless glared at her reproachfully. She fixed her father's breakfast. There came a brief lull while, standing by the sink, she drank her own coffee and ate a doughnut. "You and Eve were wonderful yesterday," her father said. "You were just great, Jen."

She hadn't sorted out her feelings yet about this triangle situation. "Thanks," she mumbled, and left to catch the bus.

When she reached school, the kids gathered around. The episode was a front-page story this morning in the Moss City Clarion. The State police had given it out, so they sounded like the heroes, but they did mention that Mr. Homer Jones, Dr. Wren, Miss Jenny Wren and Miss Eve Simmons had helped collect the animals. The police hoped that someone would come forward and give some clue to the whereabouts of Mrs. Ramona Clemm.

Jenny snorted. She had the wounds to prove she hadn't been an idle bystander while the noble police force did all the work. She had to repeat the story a dozen times. Thursa stuck to her side, puffing her up as the heroine of the occasion.

As for Hokie, he tried to be inconspicuous. His classmates' eyes brightened at the sight of him and they called, "Hey, Homer, how's it going, Homer?"

"That piece really did me in," he grumbled to Jenny when they met in chem lab. She sensed though that he knew there wasn't any real meanness in the kidding.

Thursa got off the bus with Jenny that afternoon. She was happily planning on taking home a genuine purebred Siamese cat as a present for her family. The Siamese started wailing when Jenny let them out of the bedroom, and Thursa changed her mind, fast. "My father would never put up with such a terrible noise," she said.

The girls wandered outside to see how the hospital was coming along. Mr. Caulfield was laying tile in the surgery, and his eyes bugged out when he saw Jenny's arms. "You caught it good!" he exclaimed.

"You should have seen the other guy," Jenny answered. Then she remembered; that was what Eve planned to tell her principal when she went to school today.

Hokie drove in. He put on a jumper and joined Dr. Wren, painting the office. Somebody mentioned that a cup of coffee would go down good, and the girls went back to the house to make it.

Thursa remarked that Hokie seemed to be a regular fixture in the Wren household nowadays. "He's a steady boy friend, if you want one," she told Jenny.

"I guess Hokie's okay," Jenny said. "He isn't too bad."

Thursa was arranging the coffee tray. She evidently was carried away by the thought of the Wrens' romantic twosomes. "How about Miss Simmons?" she asked. "I mean, how do you feel about her now?"

"Eve's not too bad," Jenny admitted. "I mean, there could be worse."

15

Sara Harrison called that night to tell Jenny, "My mother says I can ask you how many of the animals you and your father were stuck with."

"Why?" Jenny asked.

"We might be able to siphon off a little of the surplus population."

"We won two Siamese in the raffle and two regular cats. Our carpenter may take one of the Siamese, though."

"We'll take the other. Also I'm inviting you to a party at our house next Saturday."

"Great!" Jenny exclaimed.

"It's for my parents' friends, but if they expect my brothers and me to work like galley slaves they have to let us invite people too. You can bring a boy. See you tomorrow."

"Wait a minute," Jenny said. "What do you mean, a boy? Like Hokie?"

"Hokie bears a fair resemblance to the male sex."

"The other kids sometimes put him down," Jenny reminded her.

"Because he's slightly elongated? Other boys are fat. Or short. Or hirsute."

"You mean hairy."

"Girls too have their peculiarities, like talking for hours on Ma Bell's telephones," Sara said, and hung up.

It was no wonder the other girls resented the way Sara talked, Jenny reflected. People ought not to get so up tight, though, just because other people were different.

Like Thursa. Jenny mentioned that she was going to a party at the Harrisons and right away Thursa bristled. "I don't see how you can stand them," she said. "They're so awful."

"How are they awful?" Jenny asked.

Thursa thought a minute. "I just know they are."

"Maybe I like awful people," Jenny said. "So why do I like you? You're not awful."

"Oh, you," Thursa said, swishing her bottom primly, and they both laughed.

When Thursa got up to go, Jenny walked her half-way home. After she came back Jenny wandered out to watch Mr. Caulfield, who was painting clapboards. "It ain't gonna work," he told her, slapping his brush hard.

"What ain't gonna work?" she asked.

"That cat. It howled like a banshee. My wife's Irish so she's an expert on banshees. I promised I'd return it to you if it kept up the banshee act."

"That's okay," Jenny told him. It occurred to her that if the Harrisons were pushovers for one Siamese, they might be pushovers for two.

She picked up a broom and started to sweep up the litter inside the building. He barked at her that she was raising dust and ruining his paint job. Then he brought up the subject of the so-called Revere bowl. "I think you'd best sell it to some museum for a fancy price and knock a piece off the cost of your pa's new hospital," he told Jenny. "But that's up to you."

"Thanks a lot," Jenny said.

He caught the sarcasm and grinned. "I know your pa's sailing pretty close to the wind," he added.

Jenny was getting good at interpreting his figures of speech. "You mean the hospital is busting him," she said. "I guess we'll keep the bowl. It's always been on that sideboard, and maybe it ought to stay there. And it's not your fault if this building is busting Dad. You've tried to save money. You use every scrap of wood, and you put up with Dad's helping you, and that must be hard when you could do the job so much better." Jenny stopped, because he was gaping at her.

No wonder, she thought. She and he had started out as enemies. Then they had established a wary truce. Now she was telling the cantankerous old man that she appreciated him, and that was a terrible way to spoil a good relationship.

He put down his brush and gave her his full attention. "You're a prickly little gal," he said. "Like a porcupine. No, not like a porcupine, more like a rose with thorns. No, not like a rose, you ain't that pretty. Oh hell, I don't know!"

Jenny laughed. The outside phone bell rang, and she ran to the house, relieved that this touchy conversation had been interrupted.

A man was shouting over the wire that he was Mr.

Schuman and he wanted the doc. Jenny said the doc wasn't home, and if it was an emergency he ought to call another vet. "You his daughter?" the man demanded.

"I'm Jenny."

"That's what I did. I took your father's advice and went to another vet. I went to a young squirt named Ziller. My wife has this cat the sun rises and sets on. Or HAD this cat. It needed its teeth cleaned. Who ever heard of paying out money to get a cat's teeth cleaned? Anyway, this cat's got a violent temper. Or HAD one. So it had to be knocked out. Given an anesthetic. It up and died."

"Oh, dear," Jenny said. "I'm awfully sorry."

"It died right there on the table before that S.O.B. ever started to work on it!"

"Things like that happen," Jenny said. "Anesthesia's tricky, with a cat."

"It wouldn't have happened at your father's place."

"It could have. Dr. Ziller's a good vet."

"He's a quack, and on account of his carelessness my wife's heart is broken."

"Look, Mr. Schuman, do you want me to talk to your wife? Would that help?"

"It might. Could I come and get you? We only live a mile down the road, at the condominium."

"All right," Jenny agreed.

She went outside to wait, thinking this could be foolish or even dangerous, going off with a strange man. A big car whirled into the yard, and one look at the driver's scarlet face told her he was only angry about his cat; he wasn't setting up a situation so he could rape a young girl.

Mr. Schuman got in a few facts during the short ride. He was a retired detective from the New York police force. His wife was an invalid. He was going to sue Ziller for every cent the vet had in the world. He stopped at the entrance to Cedar View Condominiums and kept on yelling while he ushered Jenny into the apartment.

Jenny felt like crying when she saw Mrs. Schuman, a tiny woman huddled in a wheelchair like a tiny, broken bird. Jenny took her fragile hand, and somehow found the right words. She said that such things happened to every veterinarian. Occasionally people died on the operating table too, from anesthesia. The Schumans had done the right thing for their pet, only it had turned out wrong.

Jenny could see the situation. The cat was this woman's only gentle companion. Her husband obviously adored her, but he was rough, and loud. He was pacing the room now, muttering how he'd either kill Ziller or sue him, one or the other.

Jenny went on talking. "Animals do suffer," she said. "A lot of them suffer because people are cruel, but that wasn't your cat's case." To distract Mrs. Schuman she told about the incident at the mobile-home park.

A light went on then in the back of Jenny's mind. Maybe she could put two and two together and come out with more than four. "My father and I have this gray cat that desperately needs a home," she said.

"It's fur is thick and fine, like a Russian blue. We can't keep it forever, and it would be simply awful if it had to be put down after all it's been through. But at our house we already have seven cats."

Mrs. Schuman protested that she couldn't think about a new pet now, to replace her darling. "Oh, I know," Jenny said. "But when you feel you're ready, I hope you'll call us, because that cat needs a home very badly."

Mrs. Schuman thanked her, and on an impulse Jenny bent and kissed her, and left.

"How soon can we have that cat?" Mr. Schuman demanded as they set off.

"Right away," Jenny said. "But isn't it too soon?"

"I may seem like a big clumsy ox, but I do know what's best for my wife," he said grimly. "Will this cat sleep on her bed?"

"It makes a beeline for mine when it gets the chance," Jenny told him.

They went in the house. The gray cat was sitting on the sink board, washing its face. Jenny kissed its nose and carried it to the car. She tried to give a few suggestions on its care, but its new master wouldn't wait. He was clutching it and saying "Puss, puss, puss," as he drove away.

She told her father the story when he came home. "Probably I should have agreed with him, and let him sue Ziller," she finished.

"No," Dr. Wren said. "We have to earn our living in this town and the only way to do it is by playing square. And you accomplished a lot. If you can un-

load those Siamese on the Harrisons, we'll be practically in the clear again."

His "we" caught Jenny's attention. He had said, "We have to earn our living." She said, "Dad, do you really think that we'll ever get to practice veterinary medicine together, you and I?"

He was astonished. "Of course I do! What could change that?"

"Well, I just wondered. If you and Eve got married —"

"That wouldn't change a thing," he said flatly.

Oh, but it could, Jenny thought. But even if it didn't, that future seemed very dim and far away. Those seven years of expensive schooling loomed ahead, and where would the money come from?

16

Jenny was upstairs at her desk one evening that week, dawdling. She ought to be wrestling with physics and chemistry. Hokie never stopped badgering her because her grades were definitely slipping. She ought to pull up her socks and get to it, she knew that.

She heard a car turn in and went to the window of her father's room to look. This Eve, getting out of Dr. Wren's car, was the one most people saw. Probably not many had ever seen that other Eve, the witch with tumbling hair and a dirty face, swearing while she rescued cats. Now Eve's shining hair was drawn smoothly back. Her simple, green dress set off her tall figure. It struck Jenny how different she was from Martha Wren, a small, fragile woman, only five-foot-two.

Martha was very much on Jenny's mind these days. My mother was a lady and never swore, Jenny thought. What did that old-fashioned word mean, though? Anybody, looking at Eve, would certainly take her for a lady.

Dr. Wren had brought her to see how the hospital was coming along, and Jenny found them in the ward. Her father's arm was around Eve's shoulders; seeing this gave Jenny a sudden stab of pain, but she kept her voice light. "Hi," she said.

It was kind of pathetic the way Dr. Wren included her, as though he thought he had to placate her. "This tub is where Jen and I will bathe the animals," he explained. "Sometimes they need a bath or a dip for some skin disease. We'll keep the dogs and cats in cages opposite each other. Jen and I find that the cats aren't so scared if they can keep an eye on the dogs."

They wandered into the office. The painting was finished, the flooring was done, and the desk Mr. Hall had contributed gleamed with many coats of varnish. New file cabinets occupied one corner. "This is where Jen and I do our book work," the doctor went on.

"Are you good at keeping books, Eve?" Jenny asked.

"I'm a fair bookkeeper," Eve admitted.

"Maybe you'd be willing to take a look at Dad's and figure out how much money people owe him."

"No," Dr. Wren said sharply.

"No, what?" Jenny asked, startled.

"No. I've been pestered enough. It's not the animals' fault if their owners don't pay their bills."

"Humph!" Jenny snorted. She was kind of relieved, though. He wouldn't let his daughter push him around, and he apparently didn't intend to let his future wife push him around, either.

Eve went ahead into the waiting room. "Jen, will you invite her into the house?" Dr. Wren whispered.

"She can come any time she wants to," Jenny whispered back.

Eve asked about furnishing the waiting room, and Jenny explained about Mrs. Sykes. "We haven't seen the chintz. It may be awful but we have no choice; we can't hurt her feelings."

"How about a table for magazines?" Eve asked.

"We're going to use a cherry table of my mother's." Jenny noted that Eve flinched at the reference to Martha. Eve wasn't the brassy type who would ride roughshod over the memory of the first Mrs. Wren. Jenny had to give her that.

"How about magazines?" Eve went on.

"We put some out, but the customers don't find much time to read. They're too busy keeping their pets from beating up on each other."

The surgery was the only unfinished area; that was where Dr. Wren was painting now. Eben had installed the cabinets and sink. Dr. Everts would send his contribution: the fine, modern operating table. Somebody else was contributing a small refrigerator.

Jenny showed Eve the supply closet and the lavatory. She herself hadn't realized how close the hospital was to completion. "Dad, you'll be back in business in a couple of weeks. Maybe you'd better put a notice in the paper," she suggested.

They wandered outside. The clapboard exterior had its first white coat. The hand-wrought ironwork had arrived — Eben's pride and joy. Dr. Wren explained to Eve that to make Eben happy they would plant roses or honeysuckle to twine around the door.

"Eve, won't you come in the house?" Jenny invited. "We'll have coffee or tea, or whatever you'd like."

It seemed as though by now Eve would feel comfortable in the Wren house. Jenny made tea and served some nice cookies Mrs. Osborne had sent over, and did her best to be gracious. It didn't work. Eve was up tight, and soon asked Dr. Wren to take her home.

Jenny was puzzled. The last thing in the world Jenny needed was a stepmother, but lately she had been thinking that if she had to have one, it might as well be Eve. So how come Eve was hanging away?

Jenny prowled the empty house. Martha's house. She climbed the stairs, Worthless following, his nails clicking on the steps, and went into her parents' room, but didn't put on the light. She stood at the window, looking down at the floodlit yard.

She had made up a line of a poem to cover this situation, "Grief will return, again and again and again." It lessened and grew easier to bear for a while, but then it came back and washed over her with an awful force. This was one of those times.

It shamed her to remember that at first she had blamed her mother for going away. This didn't seem possible now, but it was true. After that she had blamed the impersonal, malevolent fate that had snatched a lovely and beautiful woman out of life and thrust her into the eternal dark. That resentment had vanished too, leaving in its wake only sadness.

Jenny was seeing things with special clarity tonight. Resentment had returned, she realized, and

149

now it was directed against her father. How could he turn away from Martha? How could he let another woman inside Martha's house, to sit in Martha's chair, to love Worthless, who was Martha's dog, to sleep in Martha's bed?

Suddenly Jenny couldn't bear this bedroom which had been her mother's. She went to her own, and sprawled across her bed and sobbed. Her grief frightened Worthless and he frantically burrowed, trying to push her hands away from her face. She yielded and took him into the circle of her arms.

She undressed and went to bed. She longed for sleep, which would draw a merciful curtain between her and the reality that her mother was lost forever. How could she sleep, though, when every nerve in her body was jangling? She pulled on a robe and went downstairs.

Other people seemed to get comfort out of alcohol, so why shouldn't she? She got down a drinking glass, filled it half full of whiskey, and added ice and water. The first taste made her shudder. How did people get the stuff past their noses and down their throats? She kept on, taking small sips, afraid of getting sick. Maybe eating something would help. She spread a slice of bread with butter, and things did go easier after that, and the whiskey was going to her head where it would do some good.

She finished, washed the glass, put the bottle away, and started up the stairs. The house began to pitch like a ship on a stormy sea, and she clutched the rail to save herself from falling overboard. She made it to the top and reached her bed safely. The house was swinging now in wide circles. Never again, she promised herself. What was that old gag Uncle Doc sometimes quoted, "Lips that touch liquor will never touch mine?"

At least grief had gone. If it was replaced by this awful nausea, that was an improvement. She put her light on, and that steadied the house from its wide swinging. Worthless sat on his haunches, anxiously watching her. She said solemnly, "Worthless, I am sick as a dog. Now I know how a dog feels, because Worthless, I am sick as a dog."

17

The headache woke her at six A.M., a heavy mallet banging inside her skull. Never again, she knew. She was a once in a lifetime drinker. She dressed and, holding her head carefully, descended to the kitchen.

Her father was already down. He didn't recognize a hangover when he saw one and said sympathetically, "I'm afraid you didn't sleep well." She did her morning chores and was ready before the bus arrived. Worthless saw her off, and his black eyes were twinkling. He was the only witness to her bout with the Demon Rum.

She was vaguely aware of Thursa's conversation and made the right responses. Miraculously, during the trip to school the pain began to recede. By the time they reached the high school she felt like a new woman. Not exactly bright and bushy-tailed, but okay.

She and Sara shared the same phys. ed. period, and while they were walking back after field hockey she had a chance to ask a question that bugged her. "What'll we wear, Saturday night?"

"Anything," Sara said.

"What's anything? A dress, the whole bit?"

"What did you wear to school today?"

"Jeans and a tank top."

"Wear jeans and a tank top. I'll do the same." Sara sounded annoyed because there was nothing of less importance to her than clothes. "That'll be the uniform for the evening."

When Saturday night came, Jenny gathered her freshly washed hair up in a bun, and put on a clean, red tank top and her best jeans, which were faded and frayed. Her father had a date too and was properly duded out in white shirt, tie, and jacket. "I thought Hokie was picking you up at six," he said. "You'd better get dressed."

"I am dressed," she said.

"Honey, you're going to a party!"

A car turned in, Eve's. She was picking Dr. Wren up because his car was being repaired. "Come in, Eve," he called.

He was making a big thing tonight of acting the parent, the father-figure. To Jenny's surprise he was really coming on strong. "Eve, you can settle this," he said. "Jenny's going to a big party at the Harrisons. Wouldn't she have a better time if she put on a pretty dress?"

Aha, lady! Jenny thought. You're on a spot.

Eve startled her. "No," Eve said.

Dr. Wren, startled too, demanded, "What do you mean, 'No?'"

"I mean that Jenny probably knows what the other girls will be wearing. It's dreadful to go somewhere and find you're over-dressed."

As though to contradict both Eve and Jenny, just then Hokie showed up. He stepped out of his car resplendent in neat slacks and jacket, white shirt, plain tie.

"There!" Dr. Wren exclaimed triumphantly. "Thank you, Hokie."

"For what?" Hokie wanted to know.

"For showing my daughter how to dress for a party."

"Are you going like that?" Hokie asked Jenny.

She nodded, feeling she was being backed into a corner.

"No sweat," Hokie said. He fetched a paper bag from his car. "My mother always insists that I dress up," he explained. "I keep my regular clothes in the carriage house. Where can I change, Jen?"

"Be my guest," she said happily, "Use the downstairs bedroom."

While they waited for him, Jenny asked Eve to help get the Siamese cats into the carrier. Eve held it while Jenny popped the first one in. The second witnessed its pal's fate and put up a fight, and while that was going on the first cat scrambled out. Eve and Jenny had a lively few minutes gathering in eight legs, two snarling heads, and two lashing tails, and closing the lid without pinching anybody. "We're getting good at this," Jenny noted.

"Eve ought to be," Dr. Wren said. "She worked for a humane society while she was teaching in Massachusetts."

"What did you do?" Jenny asked.

154

"I helped place animals; I cleaned cages; I did whatever needed doing," Eve told her.

Jenny made no comment, but she thought with new respect, There's more to this gal than meets the eye.

Hokie emerged. "Mrs. Harrison is going to be happy when she sees you coming," Dr. Wren said grumpily. "Two shrieking cats and a pair of bums."

"Tom, your generation gap is showing," Eve warned him.

It was a great night to be going somewhere, warm and starlit, but Jenny was nervous with the pre-party jitters. Cars crowded the Harrisons' lane, and she told Hokie to drive around to the back of the house. She tapped on the kitchen door.

Sara promptly opened it. "Now's the moment," she said. "My parents are busy out front." She took them to her room, and Jenny opened the carrier. The cats stepped out like haughty royalty, eyes fiery. "What a pair of beauties," Sara crooned.

She shut the door, to keep the beauties safe. The three joined the party.

Jenny soon felt easy and comfortable. Mrs. Harrison, wearing an Indian smock as usual, put her and Hokie right to work, passing hors d'oeuvres. They helped themselves, then carried the trays outside.

Jonas and some of his equally hairy friends were tending bar on the porch. The guests were scattered under the apple trees, where Japanese lanterns were strung. Jenny's tray was soon empty, and she went back to the kitchen for a refill. "This is quite a bash," she told Sara.

"We only give one party every summer," Sara explained. "Mom doesn't hire any help, so everybody pitches in."

Mrs. Harrison found them there. "After you finish those trays, stay and mingle," she ordered. "Join the party. You've done your chores."

Jenny took a fresh tray of tiny hot dogs in puff paste. She liked having a job to do, because how could she mingle, as Mrs. Harrison had ordered. She was scared to death of the guests.

Harley had more than its share of famous people who had moved to the country from New York, and Jenny had recognized several. These talented folk — writers, painters, theater people — shopped in the supermarkets and hardware stores, but that was all that Harley usually saw of them. Jenny moved uncertainly from group to group, and they smiled at her and went on talking.

Hokie seemed to be doing all right, he was in deep conversation with Dr. Harrison. Jenny joined them, and Dr. Harrison took her arm. Then he stopped a man who was passing. "Joe, listen to this," he ordered. "This lad has a theory."

"Sir, I don't expect you to take my ideas seriously," Hokie protested.

He explained again some theory he had. Jenny figured out they were discussing genetics. She watched Hokie's earnest, flushed face. In this dim light he was actually good-looking. Dr. Harrison and his friend listened so carefully, anyone would think Hokie was some kind of a genius.

Sara's mother came up, listened a minute, then said, "Oh, genetics. Jenny, come away. We can do better than that."

She led Jenny to a group sitting on cushions on the grass. "This is Sara's friend," she said. "Jenny Wren. Isn't it grand to know somebody who's actually named Jenny Wren?" Mrs. Harrison left her there, and moved on.

A man with a thatch of white hair got to his feet. Jenny was too flustered to place him, but thought he was a writer or a book reviewer or something. "It's really Jenny?" he asked. "Not Jane? Not Jennifer?"

"It's really Jenny," she said.

"Your mother and father knew Leigh Hunt."

"No, sir," Jenny said, "we don't know anybody by that name."

"That's not surprising, because he was a poet who lived some time ago. He wrote a little gem about a girl named Jenny," the man told her.

Jenny was stunned then, for he bent and kissed her. "I always wanted to do that," he said, and went on,

> *Jenny kissed me when we met,*
> *Jumping from the chair she sat in;*
> *Time, you thief, who love to get*
> *Sweets into your list, put that in:*
> *Say I'm weary, say I'm sad,*
> *Say that health and wealth have missed me,*
> *Say I'm growing old, but add*
> *Jenny kissed me.*

Jenny had to contradict him. "I didn't kiss you," she said, "you kissed me!"

Everybody laughed, but they weren't laughing at her; they were laughing with her. "You don't know the poem?" the man asked.

"No, sir, I never heard it before."

"My dear, you've made this evening for me," he said. "I got to kiss a Jenny, whether she kissed me back or not!"

A hand seized Jenny's. How did Hokie know she needed rescuing? He started to lead her away, but a woman said, "No, wait, Jenny. Is your father Dr. Wren, the vet?"

"Yes, he is."

"I have the pleasure of knowing him," the woman told the circle. "I took our basset to Dr. Everts last week, and Dr. Wren was there. A man had brought his coon hound in; it had been shot through the spine and was paralyzed, and the doctors had to put it down. This burly character was roaring around, really choking on his own rage. Then Dr. Wren said, sounding like an icicle, 'I can't imagine why you're upset.'

"The fellow roared, 'What the hell, somebody shot my dog!' Dr. Wren let him have it. 'You hunt,' he said. 'You're a real gun nut; you think killing's great fun. So why do you blame some other clown because he squeezed the trigger on your dog? Think about it, Buster, the next time you catch some animal in your sights!' "

The listeners applauded, and somebody called, "Good show!"

They were watching Jenny. "That's my pop," she said.

She and Hokie left then and wandered down to a wooden bridge that crossed the brook. Jenny leaned on the rail, watching the stars dancing in the water. "Thanks for rescuing me," she said. "I was kind of out of my depth."

"I was out of my depth too," Hokie said. "I decided I was making an ass of myself in front of Dr. Harrison and his friend, so I went looking for you."

"It didn't sound to me like you were making an ass of yourself," she told him. "Hokie, how come you know so much about genetics? Do you want to be a geneticist?" This question was important to Jenny. "Have you given up the idea of being a vet?" she asked.

Before he could answer they were interrupted. Sara was yelling for them to come and help get supper on.

A table on the porch was set with silver and paper plates and napkins. They lit candles in the hurricane lamps, then carried the food from the kitchen. Jenny discovered how Mrs. Harrison could entertain so many people. The supper was simple, just chili, garlic bread, and some Mexican dish made of avocados. Evidently Mrs. Harrison's chili was famous, for the guests crowded around. The kids stood behind the table and helped serve, to keep the line moving.

After everyone was taken care of, Jenny and Hokie

and Sara joined Jonas and his friends on the porch steps. No wonder people loved the Harrison parties, Jenny thought. The chili was the best she had ever eaten.

Jonas's group was talking about college, about majors and careers and job prospects. Maybe Sara decided that her own friends were being left out, because she announced, "Jenny's going to be a vet."

"So is Hokie," Jenny added. "We both thought about being vets."

The college kids were interested. Somebody said it must be great to have your career decided, so you didn't just fumble along through college. "Yes, I guess it's okay," Jenny said.

Sara caught her up on that. "What do you mean, you guess it's okay, Jen?"

Jenny couldn't admit to anybody, even to Hokie and Sara, that she didn't see how she and her father could ever hack it financially. She hesitated. Jonas, who loved argument for argument's sake, tried to pin her down. "What's changed you, Jen?" he asked. "You were certainly gung ho before. You thought everybody ought to be Saint Francis of Assisi."

Jenny was casting around for an excuse. "Well," she said, "we had sort of an awful experience lately. Hokie was there too. We went on a case with the police, some animals abandoned in a trailer."

She started to describe that day. Then she stopped. This wasn't supper conversation, and besides, these friends of Jonas's weren't all that interested. "It was a real mess," she finished lamely. "I've thought since that people are a lot better off if they don't know about things like that. Because what you don't know doesn't hurt you."

18

The party broke up at twelve. When they reached Harley, Hokie changed his mind about taking Jenny home, and turned down Main Street and parked near Town Pond.

This was always a quiet oasis at night, and the cops made frequent visits because they felt it was their duty to make sure no kids were making out in cars. They had never caught Jenny because no boy had ever brought her here. The VW was airless and stuffy, and Jenny and Hokie got out.

A thick branch of willow hung over the still pond. They edged carefully along it, and peacefully dangled their feet. Then Hokie said, "Jen, I'm worried about you. There for awhile I was nervous because your schoolwork was slipping, but you must have pulled it together because you got an A on that last hour test in physics. But now I'm worried about what you said to Jonas. You haven't really changed your mind about being a vet, have you?"

"I don't know. Maybe."

"You were happy, before."

"What does that mean? What's 'happy?' "

Hokie said patiently, "What changed your mind?"

"Well, I said what I thought. I mean, who needs it?

162

Some of the things that happen in my dad's business are hard to take. The suffering. Cruelty, stuff like that. An awful lot of people are rotten to their animals. But if I didn't have it under my nose all the time, it wouldn't bother me."

"Was it the trailer incident that turned you around?"

"No. Yes. I don't know."

"Have the police got a line on Mrs. Clemm?"

"They think so. Officer Shedd told Daddy that she has relatives in Florida, and she called one of them, and they hope she's heading in that direction. So at least they know she's alive."

"Why did what happened that Sunday turn you around?" Hokie persisted. "You were great that day."

"So was Eve Simmons. She was the great one."

"Aha," Hokie said. "We're getting down to the nitty-gritty."

"No, we aren't!" Jenny didn't want Hokie poking into her psyche. Her emotional state was precarious enough already. She slid along the tree trunk, and he clutched at her. She reached the solid ground. Hokie still had hold of her, and she thought, Hey, this is weird; I'm fighting off Hokie Jones!

He pushed her down against the grass and kissed her. His calm authority amazed her. Then he lay on the damp grass beside her, and she realized he was trembling. "Hokie, how you've changed!" she exclaimed.

It sounded as though she was making fun of him,

but he didn't take offense. He sat up and hugged his knees. They watched a sleeping swan drift by, its head tucked into its feathers. "It's getting awfully late," Jenny said. "I'd better go home."

"Jen, did you know that was the first time I ever kissed a girl?"

Maybe his male ego needed some bolstering, the machismo that boys seemed to worry so much about. "No," she said, "I thought you were some kind of an expert."

"It was."

Jenny thought she'd better match his honesty and said, "Me too. I've sort of kissed people, but not really."

"I know," he said. "I hear everybody talking around school, but I never heard anything about you making out. Not that you didn't have plenty of chances. I mean, you're sort of beautiful, Jenny."

Jenny was wishing the cops would show up and yell, "Hey, what's going on here!" She didn't like intimate conversations. When Martha died she had felt such awful grief, it had made her wary of any deep emotions. She liked things to be kept cool.

Hokie said no more, but held her against him and kissed her for a long time. Jenny was the one who was trembling now. When he stopped he said, "There!" and started to quote the same poem the white-haired man at the party had quoted, "Jenny kissed me when we met — "

She broke in, "How come you know that poem too?"

"If you weren't an illiterate, you'd know it," Hokie said. "But then, our public school system seems to encourage illiteracy."

Something was tickling her ear, and she picked a dry leaf out of her hair. "Hokie, I really ought to go home," she said, and got to her feet.

He stood up too, but instead of going to the car he led her along the footpath that edged the pond. They passed some bushes and heard rustles and giggles. They came to a bench and sat down. Hokie said, "Jenny, when we were talking to Jonas and his friends, you told them we were both thinking about being vets. Did you have it in mind that we'd get married and go into practice together?"

"That never occured to me!" Jenny exploded.

"Shhh," Hokie said. "The getting married part is okay."

"Thanks a lot. Wow! That's the best offer I've had all day." Jenny sounded scornful but she didn't feel scornful. She just didn't know how to handle this situation.

"Why don't you shut up?" Hokie suggested. "I mean it. I'm not sure, though, about being a vet. I don't know yet what field I'll go into, what I want to do with my life."

Jenny moved away from him. She was all keyed up; she couldn't concentrate on a long, philosophical discussion. She didn't answer; she just sat still. Hokie assumed she was waiting to be kissed again so he did it, holding her hard against his sturdy, skinny body.

This was dangerous; Jenny was beginning to enjoy this very, very much. She pulled away.

They wandered again along the path. The town clock bonged one. "I've got to go home," Jenny said, "no ifs, ands, or buts."

"Why are you so up tight lately?" Hokie asked. "You act as though you were threatened. Jenny, maybe you want to keep your father on a leash. You're on the defensive because you think Eve Simmons is moving in on you."

Suddenly angry, not really knowing what she was doing, Jenny raised her hand to slap him. He caught her hand. "Let's have some plain talk for a change," he suggested.

"You've got no right! You're only the hired hand who hangs around our place!"

"I'm not the hired hand because nobody pays me," Hokie pointed out. "I don't care whether I have a right or not."

"What's happened to you? You're not the same nice kid you used to be, only two, three months ago."

"I found out I was in love with you."

Jenny wanted to hear it again, and demanded, "What did you say?"

"You heard me. I fell in love with you, and I've got the horrible suspicion that it's for the rest of my life." Hokie spoke with great conviction.

Jenny thought and thought, but couldn't come up with a reply. Actually she wanted to hear Hokie repeat it some more, but instead he said, "Why do you

167

insist on disliking Miss Simmons? She's an awfully nice person."

Jenny let out a sigh. "Hokie, I don't want to go wandering around the rest of the night talking about Miss Eve Simmons." She started back along the path.

They reached the car, and Hokie put the key in the lock but didn't turn it. "Jenny, you're going to be a vet," he began.

"I don't want to talk any more."

"You're going away to college — "

Jenny shut her lips tight, refusing to speak. She was longing to be home, alone in her bed where she could think about this night and all that had been said. She leaned back in her seat, staring ahead. She was remembering Uncle Jim and his magic circles. Now she was finding herself inside a brand new one, with Hokie Jones. This was a very nice circle indeed —

They passed the baseball field, the town garage. The car bucked because Hokie drove so slowly. "Jenny, you were born to be a vet," he said. "Succoring furry things — cats, dogs, horses, rabbits — that's your bag. I don't know yet what mine is. Maybe it's genetics, or physics. Maybe it'll be medicine, either human or animal. But you'll be a vet."

The Town Hall clock was illuminated at night, and the hands were edging toward two. Hokie drove out of town and turned onto the state road. "You ARE going to marry me," he announced loudly.

"I'm done in," Jenny protested. "I can't talk any more. But you're like everybody else; you figure somebody's out of step and it has to be me."

"Has to be I," he corrected. "And you are going to marry me."

"And be Mrs. Homer Simms Jones, Jr.?" Jenny demanded. "Yecch! Who needs it?"

"Mrs. Hokie Jones," he said. "And YOU need it."

He swung into the yard. The kitchen lights were blazing and Dr. Wren stood in the doorway. "My old man looks kind of shook," Jenny said, pleased.

Hokie took tight hold of her hand and went up the steps with her. "Here's your wayward daughter, sir," he announced cheerfully.

"Where the hell have you been?" Dr. Wren barked.

"We've been the hell down by the Town Pond!" Jenny barked back.

The Wrens squared off, glaring at each other, the way they used to before their troubles started. Hokie stepped between them. "Aren't you coming on kind of strong, sir?" he asked.

"It's two o'clock in the morning!"

"So what?" Jenny demanded. "Lots of kids don't get home until six."

"You're not 'lots of kids'!"

"She's Jenny," Hokie stated. "Dr. Wren, you're making like a heavy parent."

Dr. Wren didn't stop glaring, but he said, "Hokie, you might as well get one thing straight. Jenny and I like yelling at each other. It used to scare her mother half to death."

"It doesn't mean a damn thing," Jenny said, glaring back.

"Don't you use language like that!"

169

"You use worse!"

They started to laugh. This was the way their fights always used to break up. "Hokie, go home," Dr. Wren ordered. "Jenny, go to bed."

Jenny pulled Hokie's head down and gave him a good, solid kiss. "Aha!" Dr. Wren exclaimed. "So that's what you've been doing!"

"That's what we've been doing," Hokie said. "Good night, sir. See you tomorrow, Jenny." He left.

Jenny started up the stairs, eager to be alone, longing to sort out her feelings. Actually she was dazed by her sudden happiness. She paused because she heard the buzz of telephone dialing. "Eve?" her father said in a low voice. "She's home. You asked me to let you know. Good night, see you tomorrow."

This was odd. Jenny came downstairs again. "That's odd," she said. "Don't tell me Eve was waiting up until I got home."

"That's exactly what she was doing."

"Why?"

He came right flat out with it. "She's going to be your stepmother, so she's got a right. Sit down, Jen." He heaved cats off a couple of kitchen chairs, and they faced each other across the table.

"So that's how it is," Jenny said.

"That's how. I love her and she loves me."

"She wants to move in, even knowing what it's like around here?"

"That's right. And I honestly think, Jen, she'll be a big help when you and I go into practice together."

Truth was being spoken now, in the middle of the

night. At last. It hurt Jenny to do it but she put into words her greatest fear. "Dad, we'll never be able to swing it, all those years of school. We couldn't nickel and dime that; it would take thousands."

"Eve plans to teach until you're through."

"What?"

"She'll keep on teaching. She knows the score; she knows I'm a lousy moneymaker. That's why we three will have to be partners. We need each other."

"Judas priest, Dad, that's an awful big thing!" Jenny burst out. "Her working to put me through college!"

"She doesn't see it that way. She loves teaching. She doesn't figure it's any sacrifice."

Jenny was silent. Mose was on her lap and she played with his ears. She managed to get out the most important question of all. "Dad, do you think that Eve really likes me?"

His jaw dropped. Then he closed it with a snap. "How dumb can you be, Jen?" he shouted. "Eve is nuts about you. Like everybody else! You've got an awfully hard shell, but inside you're soft as butter. It looks like Hokie has found that out. Now suppose you go to bed before you make any more stupid remarks!"

She threw her arms around him and hugged him hard, then went upstairs, Mose and Worthless and Hannibal trailing after, and she was thinking, Dumb, dumb, dumb.

She got into bed and turned out her light. That idea of Old Doc's bugged her, him and his circles. She and the cats and Worthless had one, their heads together on the pillow. She and Hokie had one now. Hey, how about that? she thought.

She and her father. Her father and Eve.

She and her father and Eve. Sleep was overcoming her, but Jenny decided, We'll be able to hack it. Inside a magic circle, hey, we might get along just great!

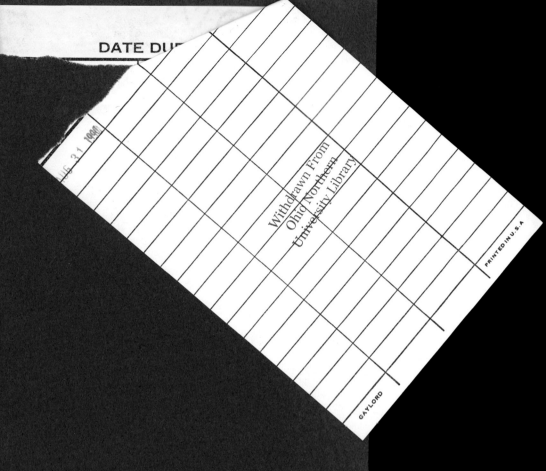